The Schoolmaster

and other stories

Anton Chekhov

Translated by
Constance Garnett

1st WORLD
LIBRARY
Literary Society

The Schoolmaster and Other Stories

Anton Chekhov

© 1st World Library – Literary Society, 2005
PO Box 2211
Fairfield, IA 52556
www.1stworldlibrary.org
First Edition

LCCN: 2006905695

Softcover ISBN: 1-4218-2124-9
Hardcover ISBN: 1-4218-2024-2
eBook ISBN: 1-4218-2224-5

Purchase *"The Schoolmaster and Other Stories"*
as a traditional bound book at:
www.1stWorldLibrary.org/purchase.asp?ISBN=1-4218-2124-9

1st World Library Literary Society is a nonprofit
organization dedicated to promoting literacy by:

- Creating a free internet library accessible from any computer worldwide.
- Hosting writing competitions and offering book publishing scholarships.

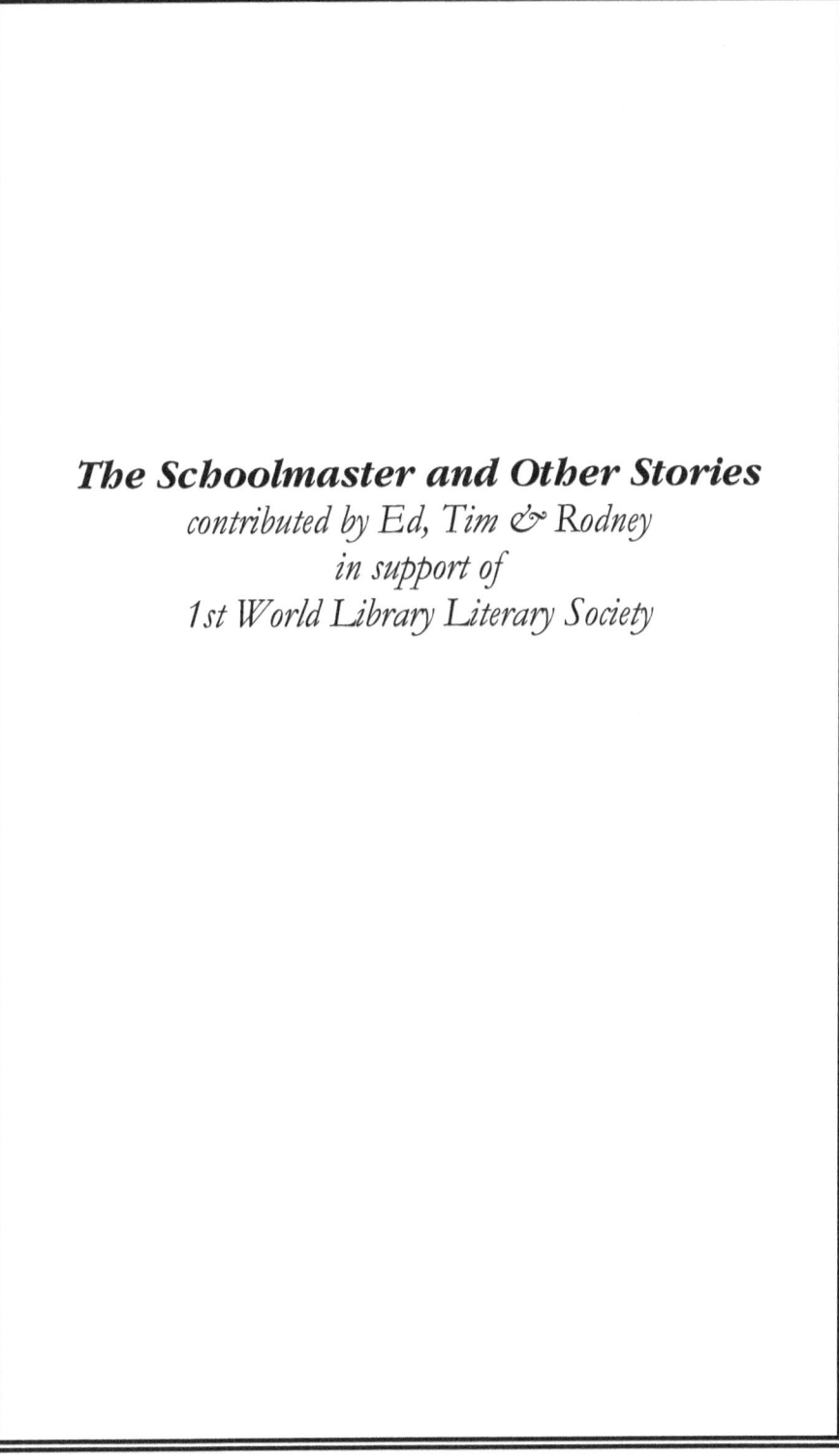

The Schoolmaster and Other Stories
contributed by Ed, Tim & Rodney
in support of
1st World Library Literary Society

CONTENTS

THE SCHOOLMASTER

FYODOR LUKITCH SYSOEV, the master of the factory school maintained at the expense of the firm of Kulikin, was getting ready for the annual dinner. Every year after the school examination the board of managers gave a dinner at which the inspector of elementary schools, all who had conducted the examinations, and all the managers and foremen of the factory were present. In spite of their official character, these dinners were always good and lively, and the guests sat a long time over them; forgetting distinctions of rank and recalling only their meritorious labours, they ate till they were full, drank amicably, chattered till they were all hoarse and parted late in the evening, deafening the whole factory settlement with their singing and the sound of their kisses. Of such dinners Sysoev had taken part in thirteen, as he had been that number of years master of the factory school.

Now, getting ready for the fourteenth, he was trying to make himself look as festive and correct as possible. He had spent a whole hour brushing his new black suit, and spent almost as long in front of a looking-glass while he put on a fashionable shirt; the studs would not go into the button-holes, and this circumstance called forth a perfect storm of complaints, threats, and reproaches addressed to his wife.

His poor wife, bustling round him, wore herself out with her efforts. And indeed he, too, was exhausted in the end. When his polished boots were brought him from the kitchen he had not strength to pull them on. He had to lie down and have a drink of water.

"How weak you have grown!" sighed his wife. "You ought not to go to this dinner at all."

"No advice, please!" the schoolmaster cut her short angrily.

He was in a very bad temper, for he had been much displeased with the recent examinations. The examinations had gone off splendidly; all the boys of the senior division had gained certificates and prizes; both the managers of the factory and the government officials were pleased with the results; but that was not enough for the schoolmaster. He was vexed that Babkin, a boy who never made a mistake in writing, had made three mistakes in the dictation; Sergeyev, another boy, had been so excited that he could not remember seventeen times thirteen; the inspector, a young and inexperienced man, had chosen a difficult article for dictation, and Lyapunov, the master of a neighbouring school, whom the inspector had asked to dictate, had not behaved like "a good comrade"; but in dictating had, as it were, swallowed the words and had not pronounced them as written.

After pulling on his boots with the assistance of his wife, and looking at himself once more in the looking-glass, the schoolmaster took his gnarled stick and set off for the dinner. Just before the factory manager's house, where the festivity was to take place, he had a little mishap. He was taken with a violent fit of coughing . . . . He was so shaken by it that the cap flew off his head and the stick dropped out of his hand; and when the school inspector and the teachers, hearing his cough, ran out of the house, he was sitting on the bottom step, bathed in perspiration.

"Fyodor Lukitch, is that you?" said the inspector, surprised. "You . . . have come?"

"Why not?"

"You ought to be at home, my dear fellow. You are not at all well to-day. . . ."

"I am just the same to-day as I was yesterday. And if my presence is not agreeable to you, I can go back."

"Oh, Fyodor Lukitch, you must not talk like that! Please come in. Why, the function is really in your honour, not ours. And we are delighted to see you. Of course we are! . . ."

Within, everything was ready for the banquet. In the big dining-room adorned with German oleographs and smelling of geraniums and varnish there were two tables, a larger one for the dinner and a smaller one for the hors-d'oeuvres. The hot light of midday faintly percolated through the lowered blinds. . . . The twilight of the room, the Swiss views on the blinds, the geraniums, the thin slices of sausage on the plates, all had a naive, girlishly-sentimental air, and it was all in keeping with the master of the house, a good-natured little German with a round little stomach and affectionate, oily little eyes. Adolf Andreyitch Bruni (that was his name) was bustling round the table of hors-d'oeuvres as zealously as though it were a house on fire, filling up the wine-glasses, loading the plates, and trying in every way to please, to amuse, and to show his friendly feelings. He clapped people on the shoulder, looked into their eyes, chuckled, rubbed his hands, in fact was as ingratiating as a friendly dog.

"Whom do I behold? Fyodor Lukitch!" he said in a jerky voice, on seeing Sysoev. "How delightful! You have come in spite of your illness. Gentlemen, let me congratulate you, Fyodor Lukitch has come!"

The school-teachers were already crowding round the table and eating the hors-d'oeuvres. Sysoev frowned; he was displeased that his colleagues had begun to eat and drink without waiting for him. He noticed among them Lyapunov, the man who had dictated at the examination, and going up to him, began:

"It was not acting like a comrade! No, indeed! Gentlemanly people don't dictate like that!"

"Good Lord, you are still harping on it!" said Lyapunov, and he frowned. "Aren't you sick of it?"

"Yes, still harping on it! My Babkin has never made mistakes! I know why you dictated like that. You simply wanted my pupils to be floored, so that your school might seem better than mine. I know all about it! . . ."

"Why are you trying to get up a quarrel?" Lyapunov snarled. "Why the devil do you pester me?"

"Come, gentlemen," interposed the inspector, making a woebegone face. "Is it worth while to get so heated over a trifle? Three mistakes . . . not one mistake . . .

Anton Chekhov

does it matter?"

"Yes, it does matter. Babkin has never made mistakes."

"He won't leave off," Lyapunov went on, snorting angrily. "He takes advantage of his position as an invalid and worries us all to death. Well, sir, I am not going to consider your being ill."

"Let my illness alone!" cried Sysoev, angrily. "What is it to do with you? They all keep repeating it at me: illness! illness! illness! . . . As though I need your sympathy! Besides, where have you picked up the notion that I am ill? I was ill before the examinations, that's true, but now I have completely recovered, there is nothing left of it but weakness."

"You have regained your health, well, thank God," said the scripture teacher, Father Nikolay, a young priest in a foppish cinnamon-coloured cassock and trousers outside his boots. "You ought to rejoice, but you are irritable and so on."

"You are a nice one, too," Sysoev interrupted him. "Questions ought to be straightforward, clear, but you kept asking riddles. That's not the thing to do!"

By combined efforts they succeeded in soothing him and making him sit down to the table. He was a long time making up his mind what to drink, and pulling a wry face drank a wine-glass of some green liqueur; then he drew a bit of pie towards him, and sulkily picked out of the inside an egg with onion on it. At the first mouthful it seemed to him that there was no salt in it. He sprinkled salt on it and at once pushed it away as the pie was too salt.

At dinner Sysoev was seated between the inspector and Bruni. After the first course the toasts began, according to the old-established custom.

"I consider it my agreeable duty," the inspector began, "to propose a vote of thanks to the absent school wardens, Daniel Petrovitch and . . . and . . . and . . ."

"And Ivan Petrovitch," Bruni prompted him.

"And Ivan Petrovitch Kulikin, who grudge no expense for the school, and I propose to drink their health. . . ."

"For my part," said Bruni, jumping up as though he had been stung, "I propose a toast to the health of the honoured inspector of elementary schools, Pavel Gennadievitch Nadarov!"

Chairs were pushed back, faces beamed with smiles, and the usual clinking of glasses began.

The third toast always fell to Sysoev. And on this occasion, too, he got up and began to speak. Looking grave and clearing his throat, he first of all announced that he had not the gift of eloquence and that he was not prepared to make a speech. Further he said that during the fourteen years that he had been schoolmaster there had been many intrigues, many underhand attacks, and even secret reports on him to the authorities, and that he knew his enemies and those who had informed against him, and he would not mention their names, "for fear of spoiling somebody's appetite"; that in spite of these intrigues the Kulikin school held the foremost place in the whole province not only from a moral, but also from a material point of view."

"Everywhere else," he said, "schoolmasters get two hundred or three hundred roubles, while I get five hundred, and moreover my house has been redecorated and even furnished at the expense of the firm. And this year all the walls have been repapered. . . ."

Further the schoolmaster enlarged on the liberality with which the pupils were provided with writing materials in the factory schools as compared with the Zemstvo and Government schools. And for all this the school was indebted, in his opinion, not to the heads of the firm, who lived abroad and scarcely knew of its existence, but to a man who, in spite of his German origin and Lutheran faith, was a Russian at heart.

Sysoev spoke at length, with pauses to get his breath and with pretensions to rhetoric, and his speech was boring and unpleasant. He several times referred to certain enemies of his, tried to drop hints, repeated himself, coughed, and flourished his fingers unbecomingly. At last he was exhausted and in a perspiration and he began talking jerkily, in a low voice as though to himself, and finished his speech not quite coherently: "And so I propose the health of Bruni, that is Adolf Andreyitch, who is here, among us . . . generally speaking . . . you understand . . ."

When he finished everyone gave a faint sigh, as though someone had sprinkled cold water and cleared the air. Bruni alone apparently had no unpleasant feeling. Beaming and rolling his sentimental eyes, the German shook Sysoev's hand with feeling and was again as friendly as a dog.

"Oh, I thank you," he said, with an emphasis on the *oh*, laying his left hand on his heart. "I am very happy that you understand me! I, with my whole heart, wish you all things good. But I ought only to observe; you exaggerate my importance. The school owes its flourishing condition only to you, my honoured friend, Fyodor Lukitch. But for you it would be in no way distinguished from other schools! You think the German is paying a compliment, the German is saying something polite. Ha-ha! No, my dear Fyodor Lukitch, I am an honest man and never make complimentary speeches. If we pay you five hundred roubles a year it is because you are valued by us. Isn't that so? Gentlemen, what I say is true, isn't it? We should not pay anyone else so much. . . . Why, a good school is an honour to the factory!"

"I must sincerely own that your school is really exceptional," said the inspector. "Don't think this is flattery. Anyway, I have never come across another like it in my life. As I sat at the examination I was full of admiration. . . . Wonderful children! They know a great deal and answer brightly, and at the same time they are somehow special, unconstrained, sincere. . . . One can see that they love you, Fyodor Lukitch. You are a schoolmaster to the marrow of your bones. You must have been born a teacher. You have all the gifts - innate vocation, long experience, and love for your work. . . . It's simply amazing, considering the weak state of your health, what energy, what understanding . . . what perseverance, do you understand, what confidence you have! Some one in the school committee said truly that you were a poet in your work. . . . Yes, a poet you are!"

And all present at the dinner began as one man talking of Sysoev's extraordinary talent. And as though a dam had been burst, there followed a flood of sincere, enthusiastic words such as men do not utter when they are restrained by prudent and cautious sobriety. Sysoev's speech and his intolerable temper and the horrid, spiteful expression on his face were all forgotten. Everyone talked freely, even the shy and silent new teachers, poverty-stricken, down-trodden youths who never spoke to the inspector without addressing him as "your honour." It was clear that in his own circle Sysoev was a person of consequence.

Having been accustomed to success and praise for the fourteen years that he had been schoolmaster, he listened with indifference to the noisy enthusiasm of his admirers.

It was Bruni who drank in the praise instead of the schoolmaster. The German caught every word, beamed, clapped his hands, and flushed modestly as though the praise referred not to the schoolmaster but to him.

"Bravo! bravo!" he shouted. "That's true! You have grasped my meaning! . . . Excellent! . . ." He looked into the schoolmaster's eyes as though he wanted to share his bliss with him. At last he could restrain himself no longer; he leapt up, and, overpowering all the other voices with his shrill little tenor, shouted:

"Gentlemen! Allow me to speak! Sh-h! To all you say I can make only one reply: the management of the factory will not be forgetful of what it owes to Fyodor Lukitch! . . ."

All were silent. Sysoev raised his eyes to the German's rosy face.

"We know how to appreciate it," Bruni went on, dropping his voice. "In response to your words I ought to tell you that . . . Fyodor Lukitch's family will be provided for and that a sum of money was placed in the bank a month ago for that object."

Sysoev looked enquiringly at the German, at his colleagues, as though unable to understand why his family should be provided for and not he himself. And at once on all the faces, in all the motionless eyes bent upon him, he read not the sympathy, not the commiseration which he could not endure, but something else, something soft, tender, but at the same time intensely sinister, like a terrible truth, something which in one instant turned him cold all over and filled his soul with unutterable despair. With a pale, distorted face he suddenly jumped up and clutched at his head. For a quarter of a minute he stood like that, stared with horror at a fixed point before him as though he saw the swiftly coming death of which Bruni was speaking, then sat down and burst into tears.

"Come, come! . . . What is it?" he heard agitated voices saying. "Water! drink a little water!"

A short time passed and the schoolmaster grew calmer, but the party did not recover their previous liveliness. The dinner ended in gloomy silence, and much earlier than on previous occasions.

When he got home Sysoev first of all looked at himself in the glass.

"Of course there was no need for me to blubber like that!" he thought, looking at his sunken cheeks and his eyes with dark rings under them. "My face is a much

Anton Chekhov

better colour to-day than yesterday. I am suffering from anemia and catarrh of the stomach, and my cough is only a stomach cough."

Reassured, he slowly began undressing, and spent a long time brushing his new black suit, then carefully folded it up and put it in the chest of drawers.

Then he went up to the table where there lay a pile of his pupils' exercise-books, and picking out Babkin's, sat down and fell to contemplating the beautiful childish handwriting. . . .

And meantime, while he was examining the exercise-books, the district doctor was sitting in the next room and telling his wife in a whisper that a man ought not to have been allowed to go out to dinner who had not in all probability more than a week to live.

ENEMIES

BETWEEN nine and ten on a dark September evening the only son of the district doctor, Kirilov, a child of six, called Andrey, died of diphtheria. Just as the doctor's wife sank on her knees by the dead child's bedside and was overwhelmed by the first rush of despair there came a sharp ring at the bell in the entry.

All the servants had been sent out of the house that morning on account of the diphtheria. Kirilov went to open the door just as he was, without his coat on, with his waistcoat unbuttoned, without wiping his wet face or his hands which were scalded with carbolic. It was dark in the entry and nothing could be distinguished in the man who came in but medium height, a white scarf, and a large, extremely pale face, so pale that its entrance seemed to make the passage lighter.

"Is the doctor at home?" the newcomer asked quickly.

"I am at home," answered Kirilov. "What do you want?"

"Oh, it's you? I am very glad," said the stranger in a tone of relief, and he began feeling in the dark for the doctor's hand, found it and squeezed it tightly in his own. "I am very . . . very glad! We are acquainted. My name is Abogin, and I had the honour of meeting you in the summer at Gnutchev's. I am very glad I have found you at home. For God's sake don't refuse to come back with me at once. . . . My wife has been taken dangerously ill. . . . And the carriage is waiting. . . ."

From the voice and gestures of the speaker it could be seen that he was in a state of great excitement. Like a man terrified by a house on fire or a mad dog, he could hardly restrain his rapid breathing and spoke quickly in a shaking voice, and there was a note of unaffected sincerity and childish alarm in his voice. As people always do who are frightened and overwhelmed, he spoke in brief, jerky sentences and uttered a great many unnecessary, irrelevant words.

"I was afraid I might not find you in," he went on. "I was in a perfect agony as I drove here. Put on your things and let us go, for God's sake. . . . This is how it happened. Alexandr Semyonovitch Paptchinsky, whom you know, came to see me. . . . We talked a little and then we sat down to tea; suddenly my wife cried out, clutched at her heart, and fell back on her chair. We carried her to bed and . . . and I rubbed her forehead with ammonia and sprinkled her with water . . . she lay as though she were dead. . . . I am afraid it is aneurism . . . . Come along . . . her father died of aneurism."

Kirilov listened and said nothing, as though he did not understand Russian.

When Abogin mentioned again Paptchinsky and his wife's father and once more began feeling in the dark for his hand the doctor shook his head and said apathetically, dragging out each word:

"Excuse me, I cannot come . . . my son died . . . five minutes ago!"

"Is it possible!" whispered Abogin, stepping back a pace. "My God, at what an unlucky moment I have come! A wonderfully unhappy day . . . wonderfully. What a coincidence. . . . It's as though it were on purpose!"

Abogin took hold of the door-handle and bowed his head. He was evidently hesitating and did not know what to do - whether to go away or to continue entreating the doctor.

"Listen," he said fervently, catching hold of Kirilov's sleeve. "I well understand your position! God is my witness that I am ashamed of attempting at such a moment to intrude on your attention, but what am I to do? Only think, to whom can I go? There is no other doctor here, you know. For God's sake come! I am not asking you for myself. . . . I am not the patient!"

A silence followed. Kirilov turned his back on Abogin, stood still a moment, and slowly walked into the drawing-room. Judging from his unsteady, mechanical step, from the attention with which he set straight the fluffy shade on the unlighted lamp in the drawing-room and glanced into a thick book lying on the table, at that instant he had no intention, no desire, was thinking of nothing and most likely did not remember that there was a stranger in the entry. The twilight and stillness of the drawing-room seemed to increase his numbness. Going out of the drawing-room into his study he raised his right foot higher than was necessary, and felt for the doorposts with his hands, and as he did so there was an air of perplexity about his whole figure as though he were in somebody else's house, or were drunk for the first time in his life and were now abandoning himself with surprise to the new sensation. A broad streak of light stretched across the bookcase on one wall of the study; this light came together with the close, heavy smell of carbolic and ether from the door into the bedroom, which stood a little way open. . . . The doctor sank into a low chair in front of the table; for a minute he stared drowsily at his books, which lay with the light on them, then got up and went into the bedroom.

Here in the bedroom reigned a dead silence. Everything to the smallest detail was eloquent of the storm that had been passed through, of exhaustion, and everything was at rest. A candle standing among a crowd of bottles, boxes, and pots on a stool and a big lamp on the chest of drawers threw a brilliant light over all the room. On the bed under the window lay a boy with open eyes and a look of wonder on his face. He did not move, but his open eyes seemed every moment growing darker and sinking further into his head. The mother was kneeling by the bed with her arms on his body and her head hidden in the bedclothes. Like the child, she did not stir; but what throbbing life was suggested in the curves of her body and in her arms! She leaned against the bed with all her being, pressing against it greedily with all her might, as though she were afraid of disturbing the peaceful and comfortable attitude she had found at last for her exhausted body. The bedclothes, the rags and bowls, the splashes of water on the floor, the little paint-brushes and spoons thrown down here and there, the white bottle of lime water, the very air, heavy and stifling - were all hushed and seemed plunged in repose.

The doctor stopped close to his wife, thrust his hands in his trouser pockets, and slanting his head on one side fixed his eyes on his son. His face bore an expression of indifference, and only from the drops that glittered on his beard it could be seen that he had just been crying.

That repellent horror which is thought of when we speak of death was absent from the room. In the numbness of everything, in the mother's attitude, in the indifference on the doctor's face there was something that attracted and touched the heart, that subtle, almost elusive beauty of human sorrow which men will not for a long time learn to understand and describe, and which it seems only music can convey. There was a feeling of beauty, too, in the austere stillness. Kirilov and his wife were silent and not weeping, as though besides the bitterness of their loss they were conscious, too, of all the tragedy of their position; just as once their youth had passed away, so now together with this boy their right to have children had gone for ever to all eternity! The doctor was forty-four, his hair was grey and he looked like an old man; his faded and invalid wife was thirty-five. Andrey was not merely the only child, but also the last child.

In contrast to his wife the doctor belonged to the class of people who at times of spiritual suffering feel a craving for movement. After standing for five minutes by his wife, he walked, raising his right foot high, from the bedroom into a little room which was half filled up by a big sofa; from there he went into the kitchen. After wandering by the stove and the cook's bed he bent down and went by a little door into the passage.

There he saw again the white scarf and the white face.

"At last," sighed Abogin, reaching towards the door-handle. "Let us go, please."

The doctor started, glanced at him, and remembered. . .

"Why, I have told you already that I can't go!" he said, growing more animated. "How strange!"

"Doctor, I am not a stone, I fully understand your position . . . I feel for you," Abogin said in an imploring voice, laying his hand on his scarf. "But I am not asking you for myself. My wife is dying. If you had heard that cry, if you had seen her face, you would understand my pertinacity. My God, I thought you had gone to get ready! Doctor, time is precious. Let us go, I entreat you."

"I cannot go," said Kirilov emphatically and he took a step into the drawing-room.

Abogin followed him and caught hold of his sleeve.

"You are in sorrow, I understand. But I'm not asking you to a case of toothache, or to a consultation, but to save a human life!" he went on entreating like a beggar. "Life comes before any personal sorrow! Come, I ask for courage, for heroism! For the love of humanity!"

"Humanity - that cuts both ways," Kirilov said irritably. "In the name of humanity I beg you not to take me. And how queer it is, really! I can hardly stand and you talk to me about humanity! I am fit for nothing just now. . . . Nothing will induce me to go, and I can't leave my wife alone. No, no. . ."

Kirilov waved his hands and staggered back.

"And . . . and don't ask me," he went on in a tone of alarm. "Excuse me. By No. XIII of the regulations I am obliged to go and you have the right to drag me by my collar . . . drag me if you like, but . . . I am not fit . . . I can't even speak . . . excuse me."

"There is no need to take that tone to me, doctor!" said Abogin, again taking the doctor by his sleeve. "What do I care about No. XIII! To force you against your will I have no right whatever. If you will, come; if you will not - God forgive you; but I am not appealing to your will, but to your feelings. A young woman is dying. You were just speaking of the death of your son. Who should understand my horror if not you?"

Abogin's voice quivered with emotion; that quiver and his tone were far more persuasive than his words. Abogin was sincere, but it was remarkable that whatever he said his words sounded stilted, soulless, and inappropriately flowery, and even seemed an outrage on the atmosphere of the doctor's home and on the woman who was somewhere dying. He felt this himself, and so, afraid of not being understood, did his utmost to put softness and tenderness into his voice so that the sincerity of his tone might prevail if his words did not. As a rule, however fine and deep a phrase may be, it only affects the indifferent, and cannot fully satisfy those who are happy or unhappy; that is why dumbness is most often the highest expression of happiness or unhappiness; lovers understand each other better when they are silent, and a fervent, passionate speech delivered by the grave only touches outsiders, while to the widow and children of the dead man it seems cold and trivial.

Anton Chekhov

Kirilov stood in silence. When Abogin uttered a few more phrases concerning the noble calling of a doctor, self-sacrifice, and so on, the doctor asked sullenly: "Is it far?"

"Something like eight or nine miles. I have capital horses, doctor! I give you my word of honour that I will get you there and back in an hour. Only one hour."

These words had more effect on Kirilov than the appeals to humanity or the noble calling of the doctor. He thought a moment and said with a sigh: "Very well, let us go!"

He went rapidly with a more certain step to his study, and afterwards came back in a long frock-coat. Abogin, greatly relieved, fidgeted round him and scraped with his feet as he helped him on with his overcoat, and went out of the house with him.

It was dark out of doors, though lighter than in the entry. The tall, stooping figure of the doctor, with his long, narrow beard and aquiline nose, stood out distinctly in the darkness. Abogin's big head and the little student's cap that barely covered it could be seen now as well as his pale face. The scarf showed white only in front, behind it was hidden by his long hair.

"Believe me, I know how to appreciate your generosity," Abogin muttered as he helped the doctor into the carriage. "We shall get there quickly. Drive as fast as you can, Luka, there's a good fellow! Please!"

The coachman drove rapidly. At first there was a row of indistinct buildings that stretched alongside the hospital yard; it was dark everywhere except for a bright light from a window that gleamed through the fence into the furthest part of the yard while three windows of the upper storey of the hospital looked paler than the surrounding air. Then the carriage drove into dense shadow; here there was the smell of dampness and mushrooms, and the sound of rustling trees; the crows, awakened by the noise of the wheels, stirred among the foliage and uttered prolonged plaintive cries as though they knew the doctor's son was dead and that Abogin's wife was ill. Then came glimpses of separate trees, of bushes; a pond, on which great black shadows were slumbering, gleamed with a sullen light - and the carriage rolled over a smooth level ground. The clamour of the crows sounded dimly far away and soon ceased altogether.

Kirilov and Abogin were silent almost all the way. Only once Abogin heaved a deep sigh and muttered:

"It's an agonizing state! One never loves those who are near one so much as when one is in danger of losing them."

And when the carriage slowly drove over the river, Kirilov started all at once as though the splash of the water had frightened him, and made a movement.

"Listen - let me go," he said miserably. "I'll come to you later. I must just send my assistant to my wife. She is alone, you know!"

Abogin did not speak. The carriage swaying from side to side and crunching over the stones drove up the sandy bank and rolled on its way. Kirilov moved restlessly and looked about him in misery. Behind them in the dim light of the stars the road could be seen and the riverside willows vanishing into the darkness. On the right lay a plain as uniform and as boundless as the sky; here and there in the distance, probably on the peat marshes, dim lights were glimmering. On the left, parallel with the road, ran a hill tufted with small bushes, and above the hill stood motionless a big, red half-moon, slightly veiled with mist and encircled by tiny clouds, which seemed to be looking round at it from all sides and watching that it did not go away.

In all nature there seemed to be a feeling of hopelessness and pain. The earth, like a ruined woman sitting alone in a dark room and trying not to think of the past, was brooding over memories of spring and summer and apathetically waiting for the inevitable winter. Wherever one looked, on all sides, nature seemed like a dark, infinitely deep, cold pit from which neither Kirilov nor Abogin nor the red half-moon could escape. . . .

The nearer the carriage got to its goal the more impatient Abogin became. He kept moving, leaping up, looking over the coachman's shoulder. And when at last the carriage stopped before the entrance, which was elegantly curtained with striped linen, and when he looked at the lighted windows of the second storey there was an audible catch in his breath.

"If anything happens . . . I shall not survive it," he said, going into the hall with the doctor, and rubbing his hands in agitation. "But there is no commotion, so everything must be going well so far," he added, listening in the stillness.

There was no sound in the hall of steps or voices and

all the house seemed asleep in spite of the lighted windows. Now the doctor and Abogin, who till then had been in darkness, could see each other clearly. The doctor was tall and stooped, was untidily dressed and not good-looking. There was an unpleasantly harsh, morose, and unfriendly look about his lips, thick as a negro's, his aquiline nose, and listless, apathetic eyes. His unkempt head and sunken temples, the premature greyness of his long, narrow beard through which his chin was visible, the pale grey hue of his skin and his careless, uncouth manners - the harshness of all this was suggestive of years of poverty, of ill fortune, of weariness with life and with men. Looking at his frigid figure one could hardly believe that this man had a wife, that he was capable of weeping over his child. Abogin presented a very different appearance. He was a thick-set, sturdy-looking, fair man with a big head and large, soft features; he was elegantly dressed in the very latest fashion. In his carriage, his closely buttoned coat, his long hair, and his face there was a suggestion of something generous, leonine; he walked with his head erect and his chest squared, he spoke in an agreeable baritone, and there was a shade of refined almost feminine elegance in the manner in which he took off his scarf and smoothed his hair. Even his paleness and the childlike terror with which he looked up at the stairs as he took off his coat did not detract from his dignity nor diminish the air of sleekness, health, and aplomb which characterized his whole figure.

"There is nobody and no sound," he said going up the stairs. "There is no commotion. God grant all is well."

He led the doctor through the hall into a big drawing-room where there was a black piano and a chandelier in a white cover; from there they both went into a very snug, pretty little drawing-room full of an agreeable, rosy twilight.

"Well, sit down here, doctor, and I . . . will be back directly. I will go and have a look and prepare them."

Kirilov was left alone. The luxury of the drawing-room, the agreeably subdued light and his own presence in the stranger's unfamiliar house, which had something of the character of an adventure, did not apparently affect him. He sat in a low chair and scrutinized his hands, which were burnt with carbolic. He only caught a passing glimpse of the bright red lamp-shade and the violoncello case, and glancing in the direction where the clock was ticking he noticed a stuffed wolf as substantial and sleek-looking as Abogin himself.

It was quiet. . . . Somewhere far away in the adjoining rooms someone uttered a loud exclamation:

"Ah!" There was a clang of a glass door, probably of a cupboard, and again all was still. After waiting five minutes Kirilov left off scrutinizing his hands and raised his eyes to the door by which Abogin had vanished.

In the doorway stood Abogin, but he was not the same as when he had gone out. The look of sleekness and refined elegance had disappeared - his face, his hands, his attitude were contorted by a revolting expression of something between horror and agonizing physical pain. His nose, his lips, his moustache, all his features were moving and seemed trying to tear themselves from his face, his eyes looked as though they were laughing with agony. . . .

Abogin took a heavy stride into the drawing-room, bent forward, moaned, and shook his fists.

"She has deceived me," he cried, with a strong emphasis on the second syllable of the verb. "Deceived me, gone away. She fell ill and sent me for the doctor only to run away with that clown Paptchinsky! My God!"

Abogin took a heavy step towards the doctor, held out his soft white fists in his face, and shaking them went on yelling:

"Gone away! Deceived me! But why this deception? My God! My God! What need of this dirty, scoundrelly trick, this diabolical, snakish farce? What have I done to her? Gone away!"

Tears gushed from his eyes. He turned on one foot and began pacing up and down the drawing-room. Now in his short coat, his fashionable narrow trousers which made his legs look disproportionately slim, with his big head and long mane he was extremely like a lion. A gleam of curiosity came into the apathetic face of the doctor. He got up and looked at Abogin.

"Excuse me, where is the patient?" he said.

"The patient! The patient!" cried Abogin, laughing, crying, and still brandishing his fists. "She is not ill, but accursed! The baseness! The vileness! The devil himself could not have imagined anything more loathsome! She sent me off that she might run away with a buffoon, a dull-witted clown, an Alphonse! Oh God, better she had died! I cannot bear it! I cannot bear it!"

The doctor drew himself up. His eyes blinked and filled with tears, his narrow beard began moving to right and to left together with his jaw.

"Allow me to ask what's the meaning of this?" he asked, looking round him with curiosity. "My child is dead, my wife is in grief alone in the whole house. . . . I myself can scarcely stand up, I have not slept for three nights. . . . And here I am forced to play a part in some vulgar farce, to play the part of a stage property! I don't . . . don't understand it!"

Abogin unclenched one fist, flung a crumpled note on the floor, and stamped on it as though it were an insect he wanted to crush.

"And I didn't see, didn't understand," he said through his clenched teeth, brandishing one fist before his face with an expression as though some one had trodden on his corns. "I did not notice that he came every day! I did not notice that he came today in a closed carriage! What did he come in a closed carriage for? And I did not see it! Noodle!"

"I don't understand . . ." muttered the doctor. "Why, what's the meaning of it? Why, it's an outrage on personal dignity, a mockery of human suffering! It's incredible. . . . It's the first time in my life I have had such an experience!"

With the dull surprise of a man who has only just realized that he has been bitterly insulted the doctor shrugged his shoulders, flung wide his arms, and not knowing what to do or to say sank helplessly into a chair.

"If you have ceased to love me and love another - so be it; but why this deceit, why this vulgar, treacherous trick?" Abogin said in a tearful voice. "What is the object of it? And what is there to justify it? And what have I done to you? Listen, doctor," he said hotly, going up to Kirilov. "You have been the involuntary witness of my misfortune and I am not going to conceal the truth from you. I swear that I loved the woman, loved her devotedly, like a slave! I have sacrificed everything for her; I have quarrelled with my own people, I have given up the service and music, I have forgiven her what I could not have forgiven my own mother or sister . . . I have never looked askance at her. . . . I have never gainsaid her in anything. Why this deception? I do not demand love, but why this loathsome duplicity? If she did not love me, why did she not say so openly, honestly, especially as she knows my views on the subject? . . ."

With tears in his eyes, trembling all over, Abogin opened his heart to the doctor with perfect sincerity. He spoke warmly, pressing both hands on his heart, exposing the secrets of his private life without the faintest hesitation, and even seemed to be glad that at last these secrets were no longer pent up in his breast. If he had talked in this way for an hour or two, and opened his heart, he would undoubtedly have felt better. Who knows, if the doctor had listened to him and had sympathized with him like a friend, he might perhaps, as often happens, have reconciled himself to his trouble without protest, without doing anything needless and absurd. . . . But what happened was quite different. While Abogin was speaking the outraged doctor perceptibly changed. The indifference and wonder on his face gradually gave way to an expression of bitter resentment, indignation, and anger.

The features of his face became even harsher, coarser, and more unpleasant. When Abogin held out before his eyes the photograph of a young woman with a handsome face as cold and expressionless as a nun's and asked him whether, looking at that face, one could conceive that it was capable of duplicity, the doctor suddenly flew out, and with flashing eyes said, rudely rapping out each word:

"What are you telling me all this for? I have no desire to hear it! I have no desire to!" he shouted and brought his fist down on the table. "I don't want your vulgar secrets! Damnation take them! Don't dare to tell me of such vulgar doings! Do you consider that I have not been insulted enough already? That I am a flunkey whom you can insult without restraint? Is that it?"

Abogin staggered back from Kirilov and stared at him in amazement.

"Why did you bring me here?" the doctor went on, his beard quivering. "If you are so puffed up with good living that you go and get married and then act a farce like this, how do I come in? What have I to do with your love affairs? Leave me in peace! Go on squeezing money out of the poor in your gentlemanly way. Make a display of humane ideas, play (the doctor looked sideways at the violoncello case) play the bassoon and the trombone, grow as fat as capons, but don't dare to insult personal dignity! If you cannot respect it, you might at least spare it your attention!"

"Excuse me, what does all this mean?" Abogin asked, flushing red.

"It means that it's base and low to play with people like

this! I am a doctor; you look upon doctors and people generally who work and don't stink of perfume and prostitution as your menials and *mauvais ton*; well, you may look upon them so, but no one has given you the right to treat a man who is suffering as a stage property!"

"How dare you say that to me!" Abogin said quietly, and his face began working again, and this time unmistakably from anger.

"No, how dared you, knowing of my sorrow, bring me here to listen to these vulgarities!" shouted the doctor, and he again banged on the table with his fist. "Who has given you the right to make a mockery of another man's sorrow?"

"You have taken leave of your senses," shouted Abogin. "It is ungenerous. I am intensely unhappy myself and . . . and . . ."

"Unhappy!" said the doctor, with a smile of contempt. "Don't utter that word, it does not concern you. The spendthrift who cannot raise a loan calls himself unhappy, too. The capon, sluggish from over-feeding, is unhappy, too. Worthless people!"

"Sir, you forget yourself," shrieked Abogin. "For saying things like that . . . people are thrashed! Do you understand?"

Abogin hurriedly felt in his side pocket, pulled out a pocket-book, and extracting two notes flung them on the table.

"Here is the fee for your visit," he said, his nostrils

dilating. "You are paid."

"How dare you offer me money?" shouted the doctor and he brushed the notes off the table on to the floor. "An insult cannot be paid for in money!"

Abogin and the doctor stood face to face, and in their wrath continued flinging undeserved insults at each other. I believe that never in their lives, even in delirium, had they uttered so much that was unjust, cruel, and absurd. The egoism of the unhappy was conspicuous in both. The unhappy are egoistic, spiteful, unjust, cruel, and less capable of under-standing each other than fools. Unhappiness does not bring people together but draws them apart, and even where one would fancy people should be united by the similarity of their sorrow, far more injustice and cruelty is generated than in comparatively placid surroundings.

"Kindly let me go home!" shouted the doctor, breathing hard.

Abogin rang the bell sharply. When no one came to answer the bell he rang again and angrily flung the bell on the floor; it fell on the carpet with a muffled sound, and uttered a plaintive note as though at the point of death. A footman came in.

"Where have you been hiding yourself, the devil take you?" His master flew at him, clenching his fists. "Where were you just now? Go and tell them to bring the victoria round for this gentleman, and order the closed carriage to be got ready for me. Stay," he cried as the footman turned to go out. "I won't have a single traitor in the house by to-morrow! Away with you all! I will engage fresh servants! Reptiles!"

Abogin and the doctor remained in silence waiting for the carriage. The first regained his expression of sleekness and his refined elegance. He paced up and down the room, tossed his head elegantly, and was evidently meditating on something. His anger had not cooled, but he tried to appear not to notice his enemy . . . . The doctor stood, leaning with one hand on the edge of the table, and looked at Abogin with that profound and somewhat cynical, ugly contempt only to be found in the eyes of sorrow and indigence when they are confronted with well-nourished comfort and elegance.

When a little later the doctor got into the victoria and drove off there was still a look of contempt in his eyes. It was dark, much darker than it had been an hour before. The red half-moon had sunk behind the hill and the clouds that had been guarding it lay in dark patches near the stars. The carriage with red lamps rattled along the road and soon overtook the doctor. It was Abogin driving off to protest, to do absurd things. . . .

All the way home the doctor thought not of his wife, nor of his Andrey, but of Abogin and the people in the house he had just left. His thoughts were unjust and inhumanly cruel. He condemned Abogin and his wife and Paptchinsky and all who lived in rosy, subdued light among sweet perfumes, and all the way home he hated and despised them till his head ached. And a firm conviction concerning those people took shape in his mind.

Time will pass and Kirilov's sorrow will pass, but that

Anton Chekhov

conviction, unjust and unworthy of the human heart, will not pass, but will remain in the doctor's mind to the grave.

THE EXAMINING MAGISTRATE

A DISTRICT doctor and an examining magistrate were driving one fine spring day to an inquest. The examining magistrate, a man of five and thirty, looked dreamily at the horses and said:

"There is a great deal that is enigmatic and obscure in nature; and even in everyday life, doctor, one must often come upon phenomena which are absolutely incapable of explanation. I know, for instance, of several strange, mysterious deaths, the cause of which only spiritualists and mystics will undertake to explain; a clear-headed man can only lift up his hands in perplexity. For example, I know of a highly cultured lady who foretold her own death and died without any apparent reason on the very day she had predicted. She said that she would die on a certain day, and she did die."

"There's no effect without a cause," said the doctor. "If there's a death there must be a cause for it. But as for predicting it there's nothing very marvellous in that. All our ladies - all our females, in fact - have a turn for prophecies and presentiments."

"Just so, but my lady, doctor, was quite a special case. There was nothing like the ladies' or other females' presentiments about her prediction and her death. She was a young woman, healthy and clever, with no superstitions of any sort. She had such clear, intelligent, honest eyes; an open, sensible face with a faint, typically Russian look of mockery in her eyes and on her lips. There was nothing of the fine lady or of the female about her, except - if you like - her beauty! She was graceful, elegant as that birch tree; she had wonderful hair. That she may be intelligible to you, I will add, too, that she was a person of the most infectious gaiety and carelessness and that intelligent, good sort of frivolity which is only found in good-natured, light-hearted people with brains. Can one talk of mysticism, spiritualism, a turn for presentiment, or anything of that sort, in this case? She used to laugh at all that."

The doctor's chaise stopped by a well. The examining magistrate and the doctor drank some water, stretched, and waited for the coachman to finish watering the horses.

"Well, what did the lady die of?" asked the doctor when the chaise was rolling along the road again.

"She died in a strange way. One fine day her husband went in to her and said that it wouldn't be amiss to sell their old coach before the spring and to buy something rather newer and lighter instead, and that it might be as well to change the left trace horse and to put Bobtchinsky (that was the name of one of her husband's horses) in the shafts.

"His wife listened to him and said:

"'Do as you think best, but it makes no difference to me now. Before the summer I shall be in the cemetery.'

"Her husband, of course, shrugged his shoulders and smiled.

"'I am not joking,' she said. 'I tell you in earnest that I shall soon be dead.'

"'What do you mean by soon?'

"'Directly after my confinement. I shall bear my child and die.'

"The husband attached no significance to these words. He did not believe in presentiments of any sort, and he knew that ladies in an interesting condition are apt to be fanciful and to give way to gloomy ideas generally. A day later his wife spoke to him again of dying immediately after her confinement, and then every day she spoke of it and he laughed and called her a silly woman, a fortune-teller, a crazy creature. Her approaching death became an *idee fixe* with his wife. When her husband would not listen to her she would go into the kitchen and talk of her death to the nurse and the cook.

"'I haven't long to live now, nurse,' she would say. 'As soon as my confinement is over I shall die. I did not want to die so early, but it seems it's my fate.'

"The nurse and the cook were in tears, of course. Sometimes the priest's wife or some lady from a neighbouring estate would come and see her and she would take them aside and open her soul to them, always harping on the same subject, her approaching death. She spoke gravely with an unpleasant smile, even with an angry face which would not allow any contradiction. She had been smart and fashionable in

Anton Chekhov

her dress, but now in view of her approaching death she became slovenly; she did not read, she did not laugh, she did not dream aloud. What was more she drove with her aunt to the cemetery and selected a spot for her tomb. Five days before her confinement she made her will. And all this, bear in mind, was done in the best of health, without the faintest hint of illness or danger. A confinement is a difficult affair and sometimes fatal, but in the case of which I am telling you every indication was favourable, and there was absolutely nothing to be afraid of. Her husband was sick of the whole business at last. He lost his temper one day at dinner and asked her:

"'Listen, Natasha, when is there going to be an end of this silliness?'

"'It's not silliness, I am in earnest.'

"'Nonsense, I advise you to give over being silly that you may not feel ashamed of it afterwards.'

"Well, the confinement came. The husband got the very best midwife from the town. It was his wife's first confinement, but it could not have gone better. When it was all over she asked to look at her baby. She looked at it and said:

"'Well, now I can die.'

"She said good-bye, shut her eyes, and half an hour later gave up her soul to God. She was fully conscious up to the last moment. Anyway when they gave her milk instead of water she whispered softly:

"'Why are you giving me milk instead of water?'

"So that is what happened. She died as she predicted."

The examining magistrate paused, gave a sigh and said:

"Come, explain why she died. I assure you on my honour, this is not invented, it's a fact."

The doctor looked at the sky meditatively.

"You ought to have had an inquest on her," he said.

"Why?"

"Why, to find out the cause of her death. She didn't die because she had predicted it. She poisoned herself most probably."

The examining magistrate turned quickly, facing the doctor, and screwing up his eyes, asked:

"And from what do you conclude that she poisoned herself?"

"I don't conclude it, but I assume it. Was she on good terms with her husband?"

"H'm, not altogether. There had been misunder-standings soon after their marriage. There were unfortunate circumstances. She had found her husband on one occasion with a lady. She soon forgave him however."

"And which came first, her husband's infidelity or her idea of dying?"

Anton Chekhov

The examining magistrate looked attentively at the doctor as though he were trying to imagine why he put that question.

"Excuse me," he said, not quite immediately. "Let me try and remember." The examining magistrate took off his hat and rubbed his forehead. "Yes, yes . . . it was very shortly after that incident that she began talking of death. Yes, yes."

"Well, there, do you see? . . . In all probability it was at that time that she made up her mind to poison herself, but, as most likely she did not want to kill her child also, she put it off till after her confinement."

"Not likely, not likely! . . . it's impossible. She forgave him at the time."

"That she forgave it quickly means that she had something bad in her mind. Young wives do not forgive quickly."

The examining magistrate gave a forced smile, and, to conceal his too noticeable agitation, began lighting a cigarette.

"Not likely, not likely," he went on. "No notion of anything of the sort being possible ever entered into my head. . . . And besides . . . he was not so much to blame as it seems. . . . He was unfaithful to her in rather a queer way, with no desire to be; he came home at night somewhat elevated, wanted to make love to somebody, his wife was in an interesting condition . . . then he came across a lady who had come to stay for three days - damnation take her - an empty-headed creature, silly and not good-looking. It couldn't be reckoned as an infidelity. His wife looked at it in that way herself and soon . . . forgave it. Nothing more was said about it. . . ."

"People don't die without a reason," said the doctor.

"That is so, of course, but all the same . . . I cannot admit that she poisoned herself. But it is strange that the idea has never struck me before! And no one thought of it! Everyone was astonished that her prediction had come to pass, and the idea . . . of such a death was far from their mind. And indeed, it cannot be that she poisoned herself! No!"

The examining magistrate pondered. The thought of the woman who had died so strangely haunted him all through the inquest. As he noted down what the doctor dictated to him he moved his eyebrows gloomily and rubbed his forehead.

"And are there really poisons that kill one in a quarter of an hour, gradually, without any pain?" he asked the doctor while the latter was opening the skull.

"Yes, there are. Morphia for instance."

"H'm, strange. I remember she used to keep something of the sort . . . . But it could hardly be."

On the way back the examining magistrate looked exhausted, he kept nervously biting his moustache, and was unwilling to talk.

"Let us go a little way on foot," he said to the doctor. "I am tired of sitting."

After walking about a hundred paces, the examining magistrate seemed to the doctor to be overcome with fatigue, as though he had been climbing up a high mountain. He stopped and, looking at the doctor with a strange look in his eyes, as though he were drunk, said:

"My God, if your theory is correct, why it's. . . it was cruel, inhuman! She poisoned herself to punish some one else! Why, was the sin so great? Oh, my God! And why did you make me a present of this damnable idea, doctor!"

The examining magistrate clutched at his head in despair, and went on:

"What I have told you was about my own wife, about myself. Oh, my God! I was to blame, I wounded her, but can it have been easier to die than to forgive? That's typical feminine logic - cruel, merciless logic. Oh, even then when she was living she was cruel! I recall it all now! It's all clear to me now!"

As the examining magistrate talked he shrugged his shoulders, then clutched at his head. He got back into the carriage, then walked again. The new idea the doctor had imparted to him seemed to have overwhelmed him, to have poisoned him; he was distracted, shattered in body and soul, and when he got back to the town he said good-bye to the doctor, declining to stay to dinner though he had promised the doctor the evening before to dine with him.

BETROTHED

I

IT was ten o'clock in the evening and the full moon was shining over the garden. In the Shumins' house an evening service celebrated at the request of the grandmother, Marfa Mihalovna, was just over, and now Nadya - she had gone into the garden for a minute - could see the table being laid for supper in the dining-room, and her grandmother bustling about in her gorgeous silk dress; Father Andrey, a chief priest of the cathedral, was talking to Nadya's mother, Nina Ivanovna, and now in the evening light through the window her mother for some reason looked very young; Andrey Andreitch, Father Andrey's son, was standing by listening attentively.

It was still and cool in the garden, and dark peaceful shadows lay on the ground. There was a sound of frogs croaking, far, far away beyond the town. There was a feeling of May, sweet May! One drew deep breaths and longed to fancy that not here but far away under the sky, above the trees, far away in the open country, in the fields and the woods, the life of spring was unfolding now, mysterious, lovely, rich and holy beyond the understanding of weak, sinful man. And for some reason one wanted to cry.

She, Nadya, was already twenty-three. Ever since she was sixteen she had been passionately dreaming of marriage and at last she was engaged to Andrey Andreitch, the young man who was standing on the other side of the window; she liked him, the wedding was already fixed for July 7, and yet there was no joy in her heart, she was sleeping badly, her spirits drooped. . . . She could hear from the open windows of the basement where the kitchen was the hurrying servants, the clatter of knives, the banging of the swing door; there was a smell of roast turkey and pickled cherries, and for some reason it seemed to her that it would be like that all her life, with no change, no end to it.

Some one came out of the house and stood on the steps; it was Alexandr Timofeitch, or, as he was always called, Sasha, who had come from Moscow ten days before and was staying with them. Years ago a distant relation of the grandmother, a gentleman's widow called Marya Petrovna, a thin, sickly little woman who had sunk into poverty, used to come to the house to ask for assistance. She had a son Sasha. It used for some reason to be said that he had talent as an artist, and when his mother died Nadya's grandmother had, for the salvation of her soul, sent him to the Komissarovsky school in Moscow; two years later he went into the school of painting, spent nearly fifteen years there, and only just managed to scrape through the leaving examination in the section of architecture. He did not set up as an architect, however, but took a job at a lithographer's. He used to come almost every year, usually very ill, to stay with Nadya's grandmother to rest and recover.

He was wearing now a frock-coat buttoned up, and

shabby canvas trousers, crumpled into creases at the bottom. And his shirt had not been ironed and he had somehow all over a look of not being fresh. He was very thin, with big eyes, long thin fingers and a swarthy bearded face, and all the same he was handsome. With the Shumins he was like one of the family, and in their house felt he was at home. And the room in which he lived when he was there had for years been called Sasha's room. Standing on the steps he saw Nadya, and went up to her.

"It's nice here," he said.

"Of course it's nice, you ought to stay here till the autumn."

"Yes, I expect it will come to that. I dare say I shall stay with you till September."

He laughed for no reason, and sat down beside her.

"I'm sitting gazing at mother," said Nadya. "She looks so young from here! My mother has her weaknesses, of course," she added, after a pause, "but still she is an exceptional woman."

"Yes, she is very nice . . ." Sasha agreed. "Your mother, in her own way of course, is a very good and sweet woman, but . . . how shall I say? I went early this morning into your kitchen and there I found four servants sleeping on the floor, no bedsteads, and rags for bedding, stench, bugs, beetles . . . it is just as it was twenty years ago, no change at all. Well, Granny, God bless her, what else can you expect of Granny? But your mother speaks French, you know, and acts in private theatricals. One would think she might understand."

As Sasha talked, he used to stretch out two long wasted fingers before the listener's face.

"It all seems somehow strange to me here, now I am out of the habit of it," he went on. "There is no making it out. Nobody ever does anything. Your mother spends the whole day walking about like a duchess, Granny does nothing either, nor you either. And your Andrey Andreitch never does anything either."

Nadya had heard this the year before and, she fancied, the year before that too, and she knew that Sasha could not make any other criticism, and in old days this had amused her, but now for some reason she felt annoyed.

"That's all stale, and I have been sick of it for ages," she said and got up. "You should think of something a little newer."

He laughed and got up too, and they went together toward the house. She, tall, handsome, and well-made, beside him looked very healthy and smartly dressed; she was conscious of this and felt sorry for him and for some reason awkward.

"And you say a great deal you should not," she said. "You've just been talking about my Andrey, but you see you don't know him."

"My Andrey. . . . Bother him, your Andrey. I am sorry for your youth."

They were already sitting down to supper as the young people went into the dining-room. The grandmother, or

Granny as she was called in the household, a very stout, plain old lady with bushy eyebrows and a little moustache, was talking loudly, and from her voice and manner of speaking it could be seen that she was the person of most importance in the house. She owned rows of shops in the market, and the old-fashioned house with columns and the garden, yet she prayed every morning that God might save her from ruin and shed tears as she did so. Her daughter-in-law, Nadya's mother, Nina Ivanovna, a fair-haired woman tightly laced in, with a pince-nez, and diamonds on every finger, Father Andrey, a lean, toothless old man whose face always looked as though he were just going to say something amusing, and his son, Andrey Andreitch, a stout and handsome young man with curly hair looking like an artist or an actor, were all talking of hypnotism.

"You will get well in a week here," said Granny, addressing Sasha. "Only you must eat more. What do you look like!" she sighed. "You are really dreadful! You are a regular prodigal son, that is what you are."

"After wasting his father's substance in riotous living," said Father Andrey slowly, with laughing eyes. "He fed with senseless beasts."

"I like my dad," said Andrey Andreitch, touching his father on the shoulder. "He is a splendid old fellow, a dear old fellow."

Everyone was silent for a space. Sasha suddenly burst out laughing and put his dinner napkin to his mouth.

"So you believe in hypnotism?" said Father Andrey to Nina Ivanovna.

"I cannot, of course, assert that I believe," answered Nina Ivanovna, assuming a very serious, even severe, expression; "but I must own that there is much that is mysterious and incomprehensible in nature."

"I quite agree with you, though I must add that religion distinctly curtails for us the domain of the mysterious."

A big and very fat turkey was served. Father Andrey and Nina Ivanovna went on with their conversation. Nina Ivanovna's diamonds glittered on her fingers, then tears began to glitter in her eyes, she grew excited.

"Though I cannot venture to argue with you," she said, "you must admit there are so many insoluble riddles in life!"

"Not one, I assure you."

After supper Andrey Andreitch played the fiddle and Nina Ivanovna accompanied him on the piano. Ten years before he had taken his degree at the university in the Faculty of Arts, but had never held any post, had no definite work, and only from time to time took part in concerts for charitable objects; and in the town he was regarded as a musician.

Andrey Andreitch played; they all listened in silence. The samovar was boiling quietly on the table and no one but Sasha was drinking tea. Then when it struck twelve a violin string suddenly broke; everyone laughed, bustled about, and began saying good-bye.

After seeing her fiance out, Nadya went upstairs where she and her mother had their rooms (the lower storey was occupied by the grandmother). They began putting the lights out below in the dining-room, while Sasha still sat on drinking tea. He always spent a long time over tea in the Moscow style, drinking as much as seven glasses at a time. For a long time after Nadya had undressed and gone to bed she could hear the servants clearing away downstairs and Granny talking angrily. At last everything was hushed, and nothing could be heard but Sasha from time to time coughing on a bass note in his room below.

II

When Nadya woke up it must have been two o'clock, it was beginning to get light. A watchman was tapping somewhere far away. She was not sleepy, and her bed felt very soft and uncomfortable. Nadya sat up in her bed and fell to thinking as she had done every night in May. Her thoughts were the same as they had been the night before, useless, persistent thoughts, always alike, of how Andrey Andreitch had begun courting her and had made her an offer, how she had accepted him and then little by little had come to appreciate the kindly, intelligent man. But for some reason now when there was hardly a month left before the wedding, she began to feel dread and uneasiness as though something vague and oppressive were before her.

"Tick-tock, tick-tock . . ." the watchman tapped lazily. ". . . Tick-tock."

Through the big old-fashioned window she could see the garden and at a little distance bushes of lilac in full flower, drowsy and lifeless from the cold; and the thick white mist was floating softly up to the lilac, trying to cover it. Drowsy rooks were cawing in the far-away trees.

"My God, why is my heart so heavy?"

Perhaps every girl felt the same before her wedding. There was no knowing! Or was it Sasha's influence? But for several years past Sasha had been repeating the same thing, like a copybook, and when he talked he seemed naive and queer. But why was it she could not get Sasha out of her head? Why was it?

The watchman left off tapping for a long while. The birds were twittering under the windows and the mist had disappeared from the garden. Everything was lighted up by the spring sunshine as by a smile. Soon the whole garden, warm and caressed by the sun, returned to life, and dewdrops like diamonds glittered on the leaves and the old neglected garden on that morning looked young and gaily decked.

Granny was already awake. Sasha's husky cough began. Nadya could hear them below, setting the samovar and moving the chairs. The hours passed slowly, Nadya had been up and walking about the garden for a long while and still the morning dragged on.

At last Nina Ivanovna appeared with a tear-stained face, carrying a glass of mineral water. She was interested in spiritualism and homeopathy, read a great deal, was fond of talking of the doubts to which she was subject, and to Nadya it seemed as though there were a deep mysterious significance in all that.

Now Nadya kissed her mother and walked beside her.

"What have you been crying about, mother?" she asked.

"Last night I was reading a story in which there is an old man and his daughter. The old man is in some office and his chief falls in love with his daughter. I have not finished it, but there was a passage which made it hard to keep from tears," said Nina Ivanovna and she sipped at her glass. "I thought of it this morning and shed tears again."

"I have been so depressed all these days," said Nadya after a pause. "Why is it I don't sleep at night!"

"I don't know, dear. When I can't sleep I shut my eyes very tightly, like this, and picture to myself Anna Karenin moving about and talking, or something historical from the ancient world. . . ."

Nadya felt that her mother did not understand her and was incapable of understanding. She felt this for the first time in her life, and it positively frightened her and made her want to hide herself; and she went away to her own room.

At two o'clock they sat down to dinner. It was Wednesday, a fast day, and so vegetable soup and bream with boiled grain were set before Granny.

To tease Granny Sasha ate his meat soup as well as the vegetable soup. He was making jokes all through dinner-time, but his jests were laboured and invariably with a moral bearing, and the effect was not at all amusing when before making some witty remark he raised his very long, thin, deathly-looking fingers; and when one remembered that he was very ill and would probably not be much longer in this world, one felt sorry for him and ready to weep.

After dinner Granny went off to her own room to lie down. Nina Ivanovna played on the piano for a little, and then she too went away.

"Oh, dear Nadya!" Sasha began his usual afternoon conversation, "if only you would listen to me! If only you would!"

She was sitting far back in an old-fashioned armchair, with her eyes shut, while he paced slowly about the room from corner to corner.

"If only you would go to the university," he said. "Only enlightened and holy people are interesting, it's only they who are wanted. The more of such people there are, the sooner the Kingdom of God will come on earth. Of your town then not one stone will be left, everything will he blown up from the foundations, everything will be changed as though by magic. And then there will be immense, magnificent houses here, wonderful gardens, marvellous fountains, remarkable people. . . . But that's not what matters most. What matters most is that the crowd, in our sense of the word, in the sense in which it exists now - that evil will not exist then, because every man will believe and every man will know what he is living for and no one will seek moral support in the crowd. Dear Nadya, darling girl, go away! Show them all that you are sick of this stagnant, grey, sinful life. Prove it to yourself at least!"

"I can't, Sasha, I'm going to be married."

"Oh nonsense! What's it for!"

They went out into the garden and walked up and down a little.

"And however that may be, my dear girl, you must think, you must realize how unclean, how immoral this idle life of yours is," Sasha went on. "Do understand that if, for instance, you and your mother and your grandmother do nothing, it means that someone else is working for you, you are eating up someone else's life, and is that clean, isn't it filthy?"

Nadya wanted to say "Yes, that is true"; she wanted to say that she understood, but tears came into her eyes, her spirits drooped, and shrinking into herself she went off to her room.

Towards evening Andrey Andreitch arrived and as usual played the fiddle for a long time. He was not given to much talk as a rule, and was fond of the fiddle, perhaps because one could be silent while playing. At eleven o'clock when he was about to go home and had put on his greatcoat, he embraced Nadya and began greedily kissing her face, her shoulders, and her hands.

"My dear, my sweet, my charmer," he muttered. "Oh how happy I am! I am beside myself with rapture!"

And it seemed to her as though she had heard that long, long ago, or had read it somewhere . . . in some old tattered novel thrown away long ago. In the dining-room Sasha was sitting at the table drinking tea with the saucer poised on his five long fingers; Granny was laying out patience; Nina Ivanovna was reading. The flame crackled in the ikon lamp and everything, it seemed, was quiet and going well. Nadya said good-night, went upstairs to her room, got into bed and fell asleep at once. But just as on the night before, almost before it was light, she woke up. She was not sleepy, there was an uneasy, oppressive feeling in her heart. She sat up with her head on her knees and thought of her fiance and her marriage. . . . She for some reason remembered that her mother had not loved her father and now had nothing and lived in complete dependence on her mother-in-law, Granny. And however much Nadya pondered she could not imagine why she had hitherto seen in her mother something special and exceptional, how it was she had not noticed that she was a simple, ordinary, unhappy woman.

And Sasha downstairs was not asleep, she could hear him coughing. He is a queer, naive man, thought Nadya, and in all his dreams, in all those marvellous gardens and wonderful fountains one felt there was something absurd. But for some reason in his naivete, in this very absurdity there was something so beautiful that as soon as she thought of the possibility of going to the university, it sent a cold thrill through her heart and her bosom and flooded them with joy and rapture.

"But better not think, better not think . . ." she whispered. "I must not think of it."

"Tick-tock," tapped the watchman somewhere far away. "Tick-tock . . . tick-tock. . . ."

III

In the middle of June Sasha suddenly felt bored and made up his mind to return to Moscow.

"I can't exist in this town," he said gloomily. "No water supply, no drains! It disgusts me to eat at dinner; the filth in the kitchen is incredible. . . ."

"Wait a little, prodigal son!" Granny tried to persuade him, speaking for some reason in a whisper, "the wedding is to be on the seventh."

"I don't want to."

"You meant to stay with us until September!"

"But now, you see, I don't want to. I must get to work."

The summer was grey and cold, the trees were wet, everything in the garden looked dejected and uninviting, it certainly did make one long to get to work. The sound of unfamiliar women's voices was heard downstairs and upstairs, there was the rattle of a sewing machine in Granny's room, they were working hard at the trousseau. Of fur coats alone, six were provided for Nadya, and the cheapest of them, in Granny's words, had cost three hundred roubles! The fuss irritated Sasha; he stayed in his own room and was cross, but everyone persuaded him to remain, and he promised not to go before the first of July.

Time passed quickly. On St. Peter's day Andrey Andreitch went with Nadya after dinner to Moscow Street to look once more at the house which had been taken and made ready for the young couple some time before. It was a house of two storeys, but so far only the upper floor had been furnished. There was in the hall a shining floor painted and parqueted, there were Viennese chairs, a piano, a violin stand; there was a smell of paint. On the wall hung a big oil painting in a gold frame - a naked lady and beside her a purple vase with a broken handle.

"An exquisite picture," said Andrey Andreitch, and he gave a respectful sigh. "It's the work of the artist Shismatchevsky."

Then there was the drawing-room with the round table, and a sofa and easy chairs upholstered in bright blue. Above the sofa was a big photograph of Father Andrey wearing a priest's velvet cap and decorations. Then they went into the dining-room in which there was a sideboard; then into the bedroom; here in the half dusk stood two bedsteads side by side, and it looked as though the bedroom had been decorated with the idea that it would always be very agreeable there and could not possibly be anything else. Andrey Andreitch led Nadya about the rooms, all the while keeping his arm round her waist; and she felt weak and conscience-stricken. She hated all the rooms, the beds, the easy chairs; she was nauseated by the naked lady. It was clear to her now that she had ceased to love Andrey Andreitch or perhaps had never loved him at all; but how to say this and to whom to say it and with what object she did not understand, and could not understand, though she was thinking about it all day and all night. . . . He held her round the waist, talked so affectionately, so modestly, was so happy, walking about this house of his; while she saw nothing in it all but vulgarity, stupid, naive, unbearable vulgarity, and his arm round her waist felt as hard and cold as an iron hoop. And every minute she was on the point of running away, bursting into sobs, throwing herself out of a window. Andrey Andreitch led her into the bathroom and here he touched a tap fixed in the wall and at once water flowed.

"What do you say to that?" he said, and laughed. "I had a tank holding two hundred gallons put in the loft, and so now we shall have water."

They walked across the yard and went out into the street and took a cab. Thick clouds of dust were blowing, and it seemed as though it were just going to rain.

"You are not cold?" said Andrey Andreitch, screwing up his eyes at the dust.

She did not answer.

"Yesterday, you remember, Sasha blamed me for doing nothing," he said, after a brief silence. "Well, he is right, absolutely right! I do nothing and can do nothing. My precious, why is it? Why is it that the very thought that I may some day fix a cockade on my cap and go into the government service is so hateful to me? Why do I feel so uncomfortable when I see a lawyer or a Latin master or a member of the Zemstvo? O Mother Russia! O Mother Russia! What a burden of idle and useless people you still carry! How many like me are upon you, long-suffering Mother!"

And from the fact that he did nothing he drew generalizations, seeing in it a sign of the times.

"When we are married let us go together into the country, my precious; there we will work! We will buy ourselves a little piece of land with a garden and a river, we will labour and watch life. Oh, how splendid that will be!"

He took off his hat, and his hair floated in the wind, while she listened to him and thought: "Good God, I wish I were home!"

When they were quite near the house they overtook Father Andrey.

"Ah, here's father coming," cried Andrey Andreitch, delighted, and he waved his hat. "I love my dad really," he said as he paid the cabman. "He's a splendid old fellow, a dear old fellow."

Nadya went into the house, feeling cross and unwell, thinking that there would be visitors all the evening, that she would have to entertain them, to smile, to listen to the fiddle, to listen to all sorts of nonsense, and to talk of nothing but the wedding.

Granny, dignified, gorgeous in her silk dress, and haughty as she always seemed before visitors, was sitting before the samovar. Father Andrey came in with his sly smile.

"I have the pleasure and blessed consolation of seeing you in health," he said to Granny, and it was hard to tell whether he was joking or speaking seriously.

IV

The wind was beating on the window and on the roof; there was a whistling sound, and in the stove the house spirit was plaintively and sullenly droning his song. It was past midnight; everyone in the house had gone to bed, but no one was asleep, and it seemed all the while to Nadya as though they were playing the fiddle below. There was a sharp bang; a shutter must have been torn off. A minute later Nina Ivanovna came in in her nightgown, with a candle.

"What was the bang, Nadya?" she asked.

Her mother, with her hair in a single plait and a timid smile on her face, looked older, plainer, smaller on that stormy night. Nadya remembered that quite a little time ago she had thought her mother an exceptional woman and had listened with pride to the things she said; and now she could not remember those things, everything that came into her mind was so feeble and useless.

In the stove was the sound of several bass voices in chorus, and she even heard "O-o-o my G-o-od!" Nadya sat on her bed, and suddenly she clutched at her hair and burst into sobs.

"Mother, mother, my own," she said. "If only you knew what is happening to me! I beg you, I beseech you, let me go away! I beseech you!"

"Where?" asked Nina Ivanovna, not understanding, and she sat down on the bedstead. "Go where?"

For a long while Nadya cried and could not utter a word.

"Let me go away from the town," she said at last. "There must not and will not be a wedding, understand that! I don't love that man . . . I can't even speak about him."

"No, my own, no!" Nina Ivanovna said quickly, terribly alarmed. "Calm yourself - it's just because you are in low spirits. It will pass, it often happens. Most likely you have had a tiff with Andrey; but lovers' quarrels always end in kisses!"

"Oh, go away, mother, oh, go away," sobbed Nadya.

"Yes," said Nina Ivanovna after a pause, "it's not long since you were a baby, a little girl, and now you are engaged to be married. In nature there is a continual transmutation of substances. Before you know where you are you will be a mother yourself and an old woman, and will have as rebellious a daughter as I have."

"My darling, my sweet, you are clever you know, you are unhappy," said Nadya. "You are very unhappy; why do you say such very dull, commonplace things? For God's sake, why?"

Nina Ivanovna tried to say something, but could not utter a word; she gave a sob and went away to her own room. The bass voices began droning in the stove again, and Nadya felt suddenly frightened. She jumped out of bed and went quickly to her mother. Nina Ivanovna, with tear-stained face, was lying in bed wrapped in a pale blue quilt and holding a book in her hands.

"Mother, listen to me!" said Nadya. "I implore you, do understand! If you would only understand how petty and degrading our life is. My eyes have been opened, and I see it all now. And what is your Andrey Andreitch? Why, he is not intelligent, mother! Merciful heavens, do understand, mother, he is stupid!"

Nina Ivanovna abruptly sat up.

"You and your grandmother torment me," she said with a sob. "I want to live! to live," she repeated, and twice she beat her little fist upon her bosom. "Let me be free! I am still young, I want to live, and you have made me an old woman between you!"

She broke into bitter tears, lay down and curled up under the quilt, and looked so small, so pitiful, so foolish. Nadya went to her room, dressed, and sitting at the window fell to waiting for the morning. She sat all night thinking, while someone seemed to be tapping on the shutters and whistling in the yard.

In the morning Granny complained that the wind had blown down all the apples in the garden, and broken down an old plum tree. It was grey, murky, cheerless, dark enough for candles; everyone complained of the cold, and the rain lashed on the windows. After tea Nadya went into Sasha's room and without saying a word knelt down before an armchair in the corner and hid her face in her hands.

"What is it?" asked Sasha.

"I can't . . ." she said. "How I could go on living here before, I can't understand, I can't conceive! I despise the man I am engaged to, I despise myself, I despise all this idle, senseless existence."

"Well, well," said Sasha, not yet grasping what was meant. "That's all right . . . that's good."

"I am sick of this life," Nadya went on. "I can't endure another day here. To-morrow I am going away. Take me with you for God's sake!"

For a minute Sasha looked at her in astonishment; at last he understood and was delighted as a child. He waved his arms and began pattering with his slippers as though he were dancing with delight.

"Splendid," he said, rubbing his hands. "My goodness, how fine that is!"

And she stared at him without blinking, with adoring eyes, as though spellbound, expecting every minute that he would say something important, something infinitely significant; he had told her nothing yet, but already it seemed to her that something new and great was opening before her which she had not known till then, and already she gazed at him full of expectation, ready to face anything, even death.

"I am going to-morrow," he said after a moment's thought. "You come to the station to see me off. . . . I'll take your things in my portmanteau, and I'll get your ticket, and when the third bell rings you get into the carriage, and we'll go off. You'll see me as far as Moscow and then go on to Petersburg alone. Have you a passport?"

"Yes."

"I can promise you, you won't regret it," said Sasha, with conviction. "You will go, you will study, and then go where fate takes you. When you turn your life upside down everything will be changed. The great thing is to turn your life upside down, and all the rest is unimportant. And so we will set off to-morrow?"

"Oh yes, for God's sake!"

It seemed to Nadya that she was very much excited, that her heart was heavier than ever before, that she would spend all the time till she went away in misery and agonizing thought; but she had hardly gone upstairs and lain down on her bed when she fell asleep at once, with traces of tears and a smile on her face, and slept soundly till evening.

V

A cab had been sent for. Nadya in her hat and overcoat went upstairs to take one more look at her mother, at all her belongings. She stood in her own room beside her still warm bed, looked about her, then went slowly in to her mother. Nina Ivanovna was asleep; it was quite still in her room. Nadya kissed her mother, smoothed her hair, stood still for a couple of minutes . . . then walked slowly downstairs.

It was raining heavily. The cabman with the hood pulled down was standing at the entrance, drenched with rain.

"There is not room for you, Nadya," said Granny, as the servants began putting in the luggage. "What an idea to see him off in such weather! You had better stop at home. Goodness, how it rains!"

Nadya tried to say something, but could not. Then Sasha helped Nadya in and covered her feet with a rug. Then he sat down beside her.

"Good luck to you! God bless you!" Granny cried from the steps. "Mind you write to us from Moscow, Sasha!"

"Right. Good-bye, Granny."

"The Queen of Heaven keep you!"

"Oh, what weather!" said Sasha.

It was only now that Nadya began to cry. Now it was

Anton Chekhov

clear to her that she certainly was going, which she had not really believed when she was saying good-bye to Granny, and when she was looking at her mother. Good-bye, town! And she suddenly thought of it all: Andrey, and his father and the new house and the naked lady with the vase; and it all no longer frightened her, nor weighed upon her, but was naive and trivial and continually retreated further away. And when they got into the railway carriage and the train began to move, all that past which had been so big and serious shrank up into something tiny, and a vast wide future which till then had scarcely been noticed began unfolding before her. The rain pattered on the carriage windows, nothing could be seen but the green fields, telegraph posts with birds sitting on the wires flitted by, and joy made her hold her breath; she thought that she was going to freedom, going to study, and this was just like what used, ages ago, to be called going off to be a free Cossack.

She laughed and cried and prayed all at once.

"It's a-all right," said Sasha, smiling. "It's a-all right."

VI

Autumn had passed and winter, too, had gone. Nadya had begun to be very homesick and thought every day of her mother and her grandmother; she thought of Sasha too. The letters that came from home were kind and gentle, and it seemed as though everything by now were forgiven and forgotten. In May after the examinations she set off for home in good health and high spirits, and stopped on the way at Moscow to see Sasha. He was just the same as the year before, with the same beard and unkempt hair, with the same large beautiful eyes, and he still wore the same coat and canvas trousers; but he looked unwell and worried, he seemed both older and thinner, and kept coughing, and for some reason he struck Nadya as grey and provincial.

"My God, Nadya has come!" he said, and laughed gaily. "My darling girl!"

They sat in the printing room, which was full of tobacco smoke, and smelt strongly, stiflingly of Indian ink and paint; then they went to his room, which also smelt of tobacco and was full of the traces of spitting; near a cold samovar stood a broken plate with dark paper on it, and there were masses of dead flies on the table and on the floor. And everything showed that Sasha ordered his personal life in a slovenly way and lived anyhow, with utter contempt for comfort, and if anyone began talking to him of his personal happiness, of his personal life, of affection for him, he would not have understood and would have only laughed.

"It is all right, everything has gone well," said Nadya

Anton Chekhov

hurriedly. "Mother came to see me in Petersburg in the autumn; she said that Granny is not angry, and only keeps going into my room and making the sign of the cross over the walls."

Sasha looked cheerful, but he kept coughing, and talked in a cracked voice, and Nadya kept looking at him, unable to decide whether he really were seriously ill or whether it were only her fancy.

"Dear Sasha," she said, "you are ill."

"No, it's nothing, I am ill, but not very . . ."

"Oh, dear!" cried Nadya, in agitation. "Why don't you go to a doctor? Why don't you take care of your health? My dear, darling Sasha," she said, and tears gushed from her eyes and for some reason there rose before her imagination Andrey Andreitch and the naked lady with the vase, and all her past which seemed now as far away as her childhood; and she began crying because Sasha no longer seemed to her so novel, so cultured, and so interesting as the year before. "Dear Sasha, you are very, very ill . . . I would do anything to make you not so pale and thin. I am so indebted to you! You can't imagine how much you have done for me, my good Sasha! In reality you are now the person nearest and dearest to me."

They sat on and talked, and now, after Nadya had spent a winter in Petersburg, Sasha, his works, his smile, his whole figure had for her a suggestion of something out of date, old-fashioned, done with long ago and perhaps already dead and buried.

"I am going down the Volga the day after tomorrow,"

said Sasha, "and then to drink koumiss. I mean to drink koumiss. A friend and his wife are going with me. His wife is a wonderful woman; I am always at her, trying to persuade her to go to the university. I want her to turn her life upside down."

After having talked they drove to the station. Sasha got her tea and apples; and when the train began moving and he waved his handkerchief at her, smiling, it could be seen even from his legs that he was very ill and would not live long.

Nadya reached her native town at midday. As she drove home from the station the streets struck her as very wide and the houses very small and squat; there were no people about, she met no one but the German piano-tuner in a rusty greatcoat. And all the houses looked as though they were covered with dust. Granny, who seemed to have grown quite old, but was as fat and plain as ever, flung her arms round Nadya and cried for a long time with her face on Nadya's shoulder, unable to tear herself away. Nina Ivanovna looked much older and plainer and seemed shrivelled up, but was still tightly laced, and still had diamonds flashing on her fingers.

"My darling," she said, trembling all over, "my darling!"

Then they sat down and cried without speaking. It was evident that both mother and grandmother realized that the past was lost and gone, never to return; they had now no position in society, no prestige as before, no right to invite visitors; so it is when in the midst of an easy careless life the police suddenly burst in at night and made a search, and it turns out that the head of the family has embezzled money or committed forgery - and goodbye then to the easy careless life for ever!

Nadya went upstairs and saw the same bed, the same windows with naive white curtains, and outside the windows the same garden, gay and noisy, bathed in sunshine. She touched the table, sat down and sank into thought. And she had a good dinner and drank tea with delicious rich cream; but something was missing, there was a sense of emptiness in the rooms and the ceilings were so low. In the evening she went to bed, covered herself up and for some reason it seemed to her to be funny lying in this snug, very soft bed.

Nina Ivanovna came in for a minute; she sat down as people who feel guilty sit down, timidly, and looking about her.

"Well, tell me, Nadya," she enquired after a brief pause, "are you contented? Quite contented?"

"Yes, mother."

Nina Ivanovna got up, made the sign of the cross over Nadya and the windows.

"I have become religious, as you see," she said. "You know I am studying philosophy now, and I am always thinking and thinking. . . . And many things have become as clear as daylight to me. It seems to me that what is above all necessary is that life should pass as it were through a prism."

"Tell me, mother, how is Granny in health?"

"She seems all right. When you went away that time

with Sasha and the telegram came from you, Granny fell on the floor as she read it; for three days she lay without moving. After that she was always praying and crying. But now she is all right again."

She got up and walked about the room.

"Tick-tock," tapped the watchman. "Tick-tock, tick-tock. . . ."

"What is above all necessary is that life should pass as it were through a prism," she said; "in other words, that life in consciousness should be analyzed into its simplest elements as into the seven primary colours, and each element must be studied separately."

What Nina Ivanovna said further and when she went away, Nadya did not hear, as she quickly fell asleep.

May passed; June came. Nadya had grown used to being at home. Granny busied herself about the samovar, heaving deep sighs. Nina Ivanovna talked in the evenings about her philosophy; she still lived in the house like a poor relation, and had to go to Granny for every farthing. There were lots of flies in the house, and the ceilings seemed to become lower and lower. Granny and Nina Ivanovna did not go out in the streets for fear of meeting Father Andrey and Andrey Andreitch. Nadya walked about the garden and the streets, looked at the grey fences, and it seemed to her that everything in the town had grown old, was out of date and was only waiting either for the end, or for the beginning of something young and fresh. Oh, if only that new, bright life would come more quickly - that life in which one will be able to face one's fate boldly and directly, to know that one is right, to be light-hearted and free! And sooner or later such a life will come. The time will come when of Granny's house, where things are so arranged that the four servants can only live in one room in filth in the basement - the time will come when of that house not a trace will remain, and it will be forgotten, no one will remember it. And Nadya's only entertainment was from the boys next door; when she walked about the garden they knocked on the fence and shouted in mockery: "Betrothed! Betrothed!"

A letter from Sasha arrived from Saratov. In his gay dancing handwriting he told them that his journey on the Volga had been a complete success, but that he had been taken rather ill in Saratov, had lost his voice, and had been for the last fortnight in the hospital. She knew what that meant, and she was overwhelmed with a foreboding that was like a conviction. And it vexed her that this foreboding and the thought of Sasha did not distress her so much as before. She had a passionate desire for life, longed to be in Petersburg, and her friendship with Sasha seemed now sweet but something far, far away! She did not sleep all night, and in the morning sat at the window, listening. And she did in fact hear voices below; Granny, greatly agitated, was asking questions rapidly. Then some one began crying. . . . When Nadya went downstairs Granny was standing in the corner, praying before the ikon and her face was tearful. A telegram lay on the table.

For some time Nadya walked up and down the room, listening to Granny's weeping; then she picked up the telegram and read it.

It announced that the previous morning Alexandr

Timofeitch, or more simply, Sasha, had died at Saratov of consumption.

Granny and Nina Ivanovna went to the church to order a memorial service, while Nadya went on walking about the rooms and thinking. She recognized clearly that her life had been turned upside down as Sasha wished; that here she was, alien, isolated, useless and that everything here was useless to her; that all the past had been torn away from her and vanished as though it had been burnt up and the ashes scattered to the winds. She went into Sasha's room and stood there for a while.

"Good-bye, dear Sasha," she thought, and before her mind rose the vista of a new, wide, spacious life, and that life, still obscure and full of mysteries, beckoned her and attracted her.

She went upstairs to her own room to pack, and next morning said good-bye to her family, and full of life and high spirits left the town - as she supposed for ever.

FROM THE DIARY OF A
VIOLENT-TEMPERED MAN

I AM a serious person and my mind is of a philosophic bent. My vocation is the study of finance. I am a student of financial law and I have chosen as the subject of my dissertation - the Past and Future of the Dog Licence. I need hardly point out that young ladies, songs, moonlight, and all that sort of silliness are entirely out of my line.

Morning. Ten o'clock. My *maman* pours me out a cup of coffee. I drink it and go out on the little balcony to set to work on my dissertation. I take a clean sheet of paper, dip the pen into the ink, and write out the title: "The Past and Future of the Dog Licence."

After thinking a little I write: "Historical Survey. We may deduce from some allusions in Herodotus and Xenophon that the origin of the tax on dogs goes back to . . . ."

But at that point I hear footsteps that strike me as highly suspicious. I look down from the balcony and see below a young lady with a long face and a long waist. Her name, I believe, is Nadenka or Varenka, it really does not matter which. She is looking for something, pretends not to have noticed me, and is humming to herself:

"Dost thou remember that song full of tenderness?"

I read through what I have written and want to continue, but the young lady pretends to have just caught sight of me, and says in a mournful voice:

"Good morning, Nikolay Andreitch. Only fancy what a misfortune I have had! I went for a walk yesterday and lost the little ball off my bracelet!"

I read through once more the opening of my dissertation, I trim up the tail of the letter "g" and mean to go on, but the young lady persists.

"Nikolay Andreitch," she says, "won't you see me home? The Karelins have such a huge dog that I simply daren't pass it alone."

There is no getting out of it. I lay down my pen and go down to her. Nadenka (or Varenka) takes my arm and we set off in the direction of her villa.

When the duty of walking arm-in-arm with a lady falls to my lot, for some reason or other I always feel like a peg with a heavy cloak hanging on it. Nadenka (or Varenka), between ourselves, of an ardent temperament (her grandfather was an Armenian), has a peculiar art of throwing her whole weight on one's arm and clinging to one's side like a leech. And so we walk along.

As we pass the Karelins', I see a huge dog, who reminds me of the dog licence. I think with despair of the work I have begun and sigh.

"What are you sighing for?" asks Nadenka (or

Varenka), and heaves a sigh herself.

Here I must digress for a moment to explain that Nadenka or Varenka (now I come to think of it, I believe I have heard her called Mashenka) imagines, I can't guess why, that I am in love with her, and therefore thinks it her duty as a humane person always to look at me with compassion and to soothe my wound with words.

"Listen," said she, stopping. "I know why you are sighing. You are in love, yes; but I beg you for the sake of our friendship to believe that the girl you love has the deepest respect for you. She cannot return your love; but is it her fault that her heart has long been another's?"

Mashenka's nose begins to swell and turn red, her eyes fill with tears: she evidently expects some answer from me, but, fortunately, at this moment we arrive. Mashenka's mamma, a good-natured woman but full of conventional ideas, is sitting on the terrace: glancing at her daughter's agitated face, she looks intently at me and sighs, as though saying to herself: "Ah, these young people! they don't even know how to keep their secrets to themselves!"

On the terrace with her are several young ladies of various colours and a retired officer who is staying in the villa next to ours. He was wounded during the last war in the left temple and the right hip. This unfortunate man is, like myself, proposing to devote the summer to literary work. He is writing the "Memoirs of a Military Man." Like me, he begins his honourable labours every morning, but before he has written more than "I was born in . . ." some Varenka or

Mashenka is sure to appear under his balcony, and the wounded hero is borne off under guard.

All the party sitting on the terrace are engaged in preparing some miserable fruit for jam. I make my bows and am about to beat a retreat, but the young ladies of various colours seize my hat with a squeal and insist on my staying. I sit down. They give me a plate of fruit and a hairpin. I begin taking the seeds out.

The young ladies of various colours talk about men: they say that So-and-So is nice-looking, that So-and-So is handsome but not nice, that somebody else is nice but ugly, and that a fourth would not have been bad-looking if his nose were not like a thimble, and so on.

"And you, *Monsieur Nicolas*," says Varenka's mamma, turning to me, "are not handsome, but you are attractive. . . . There is something about your face. . . . In men, though, it's not beauty but intelligence that matters," she adds, sighing.

The young ladies sigh, too, and drop their eyes . . . they agree that the great thing in men is not beauty but intelligence. I steal a glance sideways at a looking-glass to ascertain whether I really am attractive. I see a shaggy head, a bushy beard, moustaches, eyebrows, hair on my cheeks, hair up to my eyes, a perfect thicket with a solid nose sticking up out of it like a watch-tower. Attractive! h'm!

"But it's by the qualities of your soul, after all, that you will make your way, *Nicolas*," sighs Nadenka's mamma, as though affirming some secret and original idea of her own.

And Nadenka is sympathetically distressed on my account, but the conviction that a man passionately in love with her is sitting opposite is obviously a source of the greatest enjoyment to her.

When they have done with men, the young ladies begin talking about love. After a long conversation about love, one of the young ladies gets up and goes away. Those that remain begin to pick her to pieces. Everyone agrees that she is stupid, unbearable, ugly, and that one of her shoulder-blades sticks out in a shocking way.

But at last, thank goodness! I see our maid. My *maman* has sent her to call me in to dinner. Now I can make my escape from this uncongenial company and go back to my work. I get up and make my bows.

Varenka's *maman*, Varenka herself, and the variegated young ladies surround me, and declare that I cannot possibly go, because I promised yesterday to dine with them and go to the woods to look for mushrooms. I bow and sit down again. My soul is boiling with rage, and I feel that in another moment I may not be able to answer for myself, that there may be an explosion, but gentlemanly feeling and the fear of committing a breach of good manners compels me to obey the ladies. And I obey them.

We sit down to dinner. The wounded officer, whose wound in the temple has affected the muscles of the left cheek, eats as though he had a bit in his mouth. I roll up little balls of bread, think about the dog licence, and, knowing the ungovernable violence of my temper, try to avoid speaking. Nadenka looks at me sympathetically.

Soup, tongue and peas, roast fowl, and compote. I have no appetite, but eat from politeness.

After dinner, while I am standing alone on the terrace, smoking, Nadenka's mamma comes up to me, presses my hand, and says breathlessly:

"Don't despair, *Nicolas!* She has such a heart, . . . such a heart! . . ."

We go towards the wood to gather mushrooms. Varenka hangs on my arm and clings to my side. My sufferings are indescribable, but I bear them in patience.

We enter the wood.

"Listen, Monsieur Nicolas," says Nadenka, sighing. "Why are you so melancholy? And why are you so silent?"

Extraordinary girl she is, really! What can I talk to her about? What have we in common?

"Oh, do say something!" she begs me.

I begin trying to think of something popular, something within the range of her understanding. After a moment's thought I say:

"The cutting down of forests has been greatly detrimental to the prosperity of Russia. . . ."

"Nicolas," sighs Nadenka, and her nose begins to turn red, "Nicolas, I see you are trying to avoid being open with me. . . . You seem to wish to punish me by your

Anton Chekhov

silence. Your feeling is not returned, and you wish to suffer in silence, in solitude . . . it is too awful, Nicolas!" she cries impulsively seizing my hand, and I see her nose beginning to swell. "What would you say if the girl you love were to offer you her eternal friendship?"

I mutter something incoherent, for I really can't think what to say to her.

In the first place, I'm not in love with any girl at all; in the second, what could I possibly want her eternal friendship for? and, thirdly, I have a violent temper.

Mashenka (or Varenka) hides her face in her hands and murmurs, as though to herself:

"He will not speak; . . . it is clear that he will have me make the sacrifice! I cannot love him, if my heart is still another's . . . but . . . I will think of it. . . . Very good, I will think of it . . . I will prove the strength of my soul, and perhaps, at the cost of my own happiness, I will save this man from suffering!" . . .

I can make nothing out of all this. It seems some special sort of puzzle.

We go farther into the wood and begin picking mushrooms. We are perfectly silent the whole time. Nadenka's face shows signs of inward struggle. I hear the bark of dogs; it reminds me of my dissertation, and I sigh heavily. Between the trees I catch sight of the wounded officer limping painfully along. The poor fellow's right leg is lame from his wound, and on his left arm he has one of the variegated young ladies. His face expresses resignation to destiny.

We go back to the house to drink tea, after which we play croquet and listen to one of the variegated young ladies singing a song: "No, no, thou lovest not, no, no." At the word "no" she twists her mouth till it almost touches one ear.

"*Charmant!*" wail the other young ladies, "*Charmant!*"

The evening comes on. A detestable moon creeps up behind the bushes. There is perfect stillness in the air, and an unpleasant smell of freshly cut hay. I take up my hat and try to get away.

"I have something I must say to you!" Mashenka whispers to me significantly, "don't go away!"

I have a foreboding of evil, but politeness obliges me to remain. Mashenka takes my arm and leads me away to a garden walk. By this time her whole figure expresses conflict. She is pale and gasping for breath, and she seems absolutely set on pulling my right arm out of the socket. What can be the matter with her?

"Listen!" she mutters. "No, I cannot! No! . . ." She tries to say something, but hesitates. Now I see from her face that she has come to some decision. With gleaming eyes and swollen nose she snatches my hand, and says hurriedly, "*Nicolas*, I am yours! Love you I cannot, but I promise to be true to you!"

Then she squeezes herself to my breast, and at once springs away.

"Someone is coming," she whispers. "Farewell! . . . To-morrow at eleven o'clock I will be in the arbour. . . Farewell!"

And she vanishes. Completely at a loss for an explanation of her conduct and suffering from a painful palpitation of the heart, I make my way home. There the "Past and Future of the Dog Licence" is awaiting me, but I am quite unable to work. I am furious. . . . I may say, my anger is terrible. Damn it all! I allow no one to treat me like a boy, I am a man of violent temper, and it is not safe to trifle with me!

When the maid comes in to call me to supper, I shout to her: "Go out of the room!" Such hastiness augurs nothing good.

Next morning. Typical holiday weather. Temperature below freezing, a cutting wind, rain, mud, and a smell of naphthaline, because my *maman* has taken all her wraps out of her trunks. A devilish morning! It is the 7th of August, 1887, the date of the solar eclipse. I may here remark that at the time of an eclipse every one of us may, without special astronomical know-ledge, be of the greatest service. Thus, for example, anyone of us can (1) take the measurement of the diameters of the sun and the moon; (2) sketch the corona of the sun; (3) take the temperature; (4) take observations of plants and animals during the eclipse; (5) note down his own impressions, and so on.

It is a matter of such exceptional importance that I lay aside the "Past and Future of the Dog Licence" and make up my mind to observe the eclipse.

We all get up very early, and I divide the work as follows: I am to measure the diameter of the sun and moon; the wounded officer is to sketch the corona; and the other observations are undertaken by Mashenka and the variegated young ladies.

We all meet together and wait.

"What is the cause of the eclipse?" asks Mashenka.

I reply: "A solar eclipse occurs when the moon, moving in the plane of the ecliptic, crosses the line joining the centres of the sun and the earth."

"And what does the ecliptic mean?"

I explain. Mashenka listens attentively.

"Can one see through the smoked glass the line joining the centres of the sun and the earth?" she enquires.

I reply that this is only an imaginary line, drawn theoretically.

"If it is only an imaginary line, how can the moon cross it?" Varenka says, wondering.

I make no reply. I feel my spleen rising at this naive question.

"It's all nonsense," says Mashenka's *maman*. "Impossible to tell what's going to happen. You've never been in the sky, so what can you know of what is to happen with the sun and moon? It's all fancy."

At that moment a black patch begins to move over the sun. General confusion follows. The sheep and horses and cows run bellowing about the fields with their tails in the air. The dogs howl. The bugs, thinking night has come on, creep out of the cracks in the walls and bite the people who are still in bed.

Anton Chekhov

The deacon, who was engaged in bringing some cucumbers from the market garden, jumped out of his cart and hid under the bridge; while his horse walked off into somebody else's yard, where the pigs ate up all the cucumbers. The excise officer, who had not slept at home that night, but at a lady friend's, dashed out with nothing on but his nightshirt, and running into the crowd shouted frantically: "Save yourself, if you can!"

Numbers of the lady visitors, even young and pretty ones, run out of their villas without even putting their slippers on. Scenes occur which I hesitate to describe.

"Oh, how dreadful!" shriek the variegated young ladies. "It's really too awful!"

"Mesdames, watch!" I cry. "Time is precious!"

And I hasten to measure the diameters. I remember the corona, and look towards the wounded officer. He stands doing nothing.

"What's the matter?" I shout. "How about the corona?"

He shrugs his shoulders and looks helplessly towards his arms. The poor fellow has variegated young ladies on both sides of him, clinging to him in terror and preventing him from working. I seize a pencil and note down the time to a second. That is of great importance. I note down the geographical position of the point of observation. That, too, is of importance. I am just about to measure the diameter when Mashenka seizes my hand, and says:

"Do not forget to-day, eleven o'clock."

I withdraw my hand, feeling every second precious, try to continue my observations, but Varenka clutches my arm and clings to me. Pencil, pieces of glass, drawings - all are scattered on the grass. Hang it! It's high time the girl realized that I am a man of violent temper, and when I am roused my fury knows no bounds, I cannot answer for myself.

I try to continue, but the eclipse is over.

"Look at me!" she whispers tenderly.

Oh, that is the last straw! Trying a man's patience like that can but have a fatal ending. I am not to blame if something terrible happens. I allow no one to make a laughing stock of me, and, God knows, when I am furious, I advise nobody to come near me, damn it all! There's nothing I might not do! One of the young ladies, probably noticing from my face what a rage I am in, and anxious to propitiate me, says:

"I did exactly what you told me, Nikolay Andreitch; I watched the animals. I saw the grey dog chasing the cat just before the eclipse, and wagging his tail for a long while afterwards."

So nothing came of the eclipse after all.

I go home. Thanks to the rain, I work indoors instead of on the balcony. The wounded officer has risked it, and has again got as far as "I was born in . . ." when I see one of the variegated young ladies pounce down on him and bear him off to her villa.

I cannot work, for I am still in a fury and suffering from palpitation of the heart. I do not go to the arbour.

It is impolite not to, but, after all, I can't be expected to go in the rain.

At twelve o'clock I receive a letter from Mashenka, a letter full of reproaches and entreaties to go to the arbour, addressing me as "thou." At one o'clock I get a second letter, and at two, a third . . . . I must go. . . . But before going I must consider what I am to say to her. I will behave like a gentleman.

To begin with, I will tell her that she is mistaken in supposing that I am in love with her. That's a thing one does not say to a lady as a rule, though. To tell a lady that one's not in love with her, is almost as rude as to tell an author he can't write.

The best thing will be to explain my views of marriage.

I put on my winter overcoat, take an umbrella, and walk to the arbour.

Knowing the hastiness of my temper, I am afraid I may be led into speaking too strongly; I will try to restrain myself.

I find Nadenka still waiting for me. She is pale and in tears. On seeing me she utters a cry of joy, flings herself on my neck, and says:

"At last! You are trying my patience. . . . Listen, I have not slept all night. . . . I have been thinking and thinking. . . . I believe that when I come to know you better I shall learn to love you. . . ."

I sit down, and begin to unfold my views of marriage. To begin with, to clear the ground of digressions and to be as brief as possible, I open with a short historical survey. I speak of marriage in ancient Egypt and India, then pass to more recent times, a few ideas from Schopenhauer. Mashenka listens attentively, but all of a sudden, through some strange incoherence of ideas, thinks fit to interrupt me:

"Nicolas, kiss me!" she says.

I am embarrassed and don't know what to say to her. She repeats her request. There seems no avoiding it. I get up and bend over her long face, feeling as I do so just as I did in my childhood when I was lifted up to kiss my grandmother in her coffin. Not content with the kiss, Mashenka leaps up and impulsively embraces me. At that instant, Mashenka's *maman* appears in the doorway of the arbour. . . . She makes a face as though in alarm, and saying "sh-sh" to someone with her, vanishes like Mephistopheles through the trapdoor.

Confused and enraged, I return to our villa. At home I find Varenka's *maman* embracing my *maman* with tears in her eyes. And my *maman* weeps and says:

"I always hoped for it!"

And then, if you please, Nadenka's *maman* comes up to me, embraces me, and says:

"May God bless you! . . . Mind you love her well. . . . Remember the sacrifice she is making for your sake!"

And here I am at my wedding. At the moment I write these last words, my best man is at my side, urging me to make haste. These people have no idea of my character! I have a violent temper, I cannot always answer for myself! Hang it all! God knows what will come of it! To lead a violent, desperate man to the altar is as unwise as to thrust one's hand into the cage of a ferocious tiger. We shall see, we shall see!

* * * * *

And so, I am married. Everybody congratulates me and Varenka keeps clinging to me and saying:

"Now you are mine, mine; do you understand that? Tell me that you love me!" And her nose swells as she says it.

I learn from my best man that the wounded officer has very cleverly escaped the snares of Hymen. He showed the variegated young lady a medical certificate that owing to the wound in his temple he was at times mentally deranged and incapable of contracting a valid marriage. An inspiration! I might have got a certificate too. An uncle of mine drank himself to death, another uncle was extremely absent-minded (on one occasion he put a lady's muff on his head in mistake for his hat), an aunt of mine played a great deal on the piano, and used to put out her tongue at gentlemen she did not like. And my ungovernable temper is a very suspicious symptom.

But why do these great ideas always come too late? Why?

IN THE DARK

A FLY of medium size made its way into the nose of the assistant procurator, Gagin. It may have been impelled by curiosity, or have got there through frivolity or accident in the dark; anyway, the nose resented the presence of a foreign body and gave the signal for a sneeze. Gagin sneezed, sneezed impressively and so shrilly and loudly that the bed shook and the springs creaked. Gagin's wife, Marya Mihalovna, a full, plump, fair woman, started, too, and woke up. She gazed into the darkness, sighed, and turned over on the other side. Five minutes afterwards she turned over again and shut her eyes more firmly but she could not get to sleep again. After sighing and tossing from side to side for a time, she got up, crept over her husband, and putting on her slippers, went to the window.

It was dark outside. She could see nothing but the outlines of the trees and the roof of the stables. There was a faint pallor in the east, but this pallor was beginning to be clouded over. There was perfect stillness in the air wrapped in slumber and darkness. Even the watchman, paid to disturb the stillness of night, was silent; even the corncrake - the only wild creature of the feathered tribe that does not shun the proximity of summer visitors - was silent.

Anton Chekhov

The stillness was broken by Marya Mihalovna herself. Standing at the window and gazing into the yard, she suddenly uttered a cry. She fancied that from the flower garden with the gaunt, clipped poplar, a dark figure was creeping towards the house. For the first minute she thought it was a cow or a horse, then, rubbing her eyes, she distinguished clearly the outlines of a man.

Then she fancied the dark figure approached the window of the kitchen and, standing still a moment, apparently undecided, put one foot on the window ledge and disappeared into the darkness of the window.

"A burglar!" flashed into her mind and a deathly pallor overspread her face.

And in one instant her imagination had drawn the picture so dreaded by lady visitors in country places - a burglar creeps into the kitchen, from the kitchen into the dining-room . . . the silver in the cupboard . . . next into the bedroom . . . an axe . . . the face of a brigand . . . jewelry. . . . Her knees gave way under her and a shiver ran down her back.

"Vassya!" she said, shaking her husband, "*Basile!* Vassily Prokovitch! Ah! mercy on us, he might be dead! Wake up, *Basile*, I beseech you!"

"W-well?" grunted the assistant procurator, with a deep inward breath and a munching sound.

"For God's sake, wake up! A burglar has got into the kitchen! I was standing at the window looking out and someone got in at the window. He will get into the dining-room next . . . the spoons are in the cupboard!

Basile! They broke into Mavra Yegorovna's last year."

"Wha - what's the matter?"

"Heavens! he does not understand. Do listen, you stupid! I tell you I've just seen a man getting in at the kitchen window! Pelagea will be frightened and . . . and the silver is in the cupboard!"

"Stuff and nonsense!"

"*Basile* , this is unbearable! I tell you of a real danger and you sleep and grunt! What would you have? Would you have us robbed and murdered?"

The assistant procurator slowly got up and sat on the bed, filling the air with loud yawns.

"Goodness knows what creatures women are!" he muttered. "Can't leave one in peace even at night! To wake a man for such nonsense!"

"But, *Basile* , I swear I saw a man getting in at the window!"

"Well, what of it? Let him get in. . . . That's pretty sure to be Pelagea's sweetheart, the fireman."

"What! what did you say?"

"I say it's Pelagea's fireman come to see her."

"Worse than ever!" shrieked Marya Mihalovna. "That's worse than a burglar! I won't put up with cynicism in my house!"

Anton Chekhov

"Hoity-toity! We are virtuous! . . . Won't put up with cynicism? As though it were cynicism! What's the use of firing off those foreign words? My dear girl, it's a thing that has happened ever since the world began, sanctified by tradition. What's a fireman for if not to make love to the cook?"

"No, *Basile!* It seems you don't know me! I cannot face the idea of such a . . . such a . . . in my house. You must go this minute into the kitchen and tell him to go away! This very minute! And to-morrow I'll tell Pelagea that she must not dare to demean herself by such proceedings! When I am dead you may allow immorality in your house, but you shan't do it now! . . . Please go!"

"Damn it," grumbled Gagin, annoyed. "Consider with your microscopic female brain, what am I to go for?"

"*Basile,* I shall faint! . . ."

Gagin cursed, put on his slippers, cursed again, and set off to the kitchen. It was as dark as the inside of a barrel, and the assistant procurator had to feel his way. He groped his way to the door of the nursery and waked the nurse.

"Vassilissa," he said, "you took my dressing-gown to brush last night - where is it?"

"I gave it to Pelagea to brush, sir."

"What carelessness! You take it away and don't put it back - now I've to go without a dressing-gown!"

On reaching the kitchen, he made his way to the corner

in which on a box under a shelf of saucepans the cook slept.

"Pelagea," he said, feeling her shoulder and giving it a shake, "Pelagea! Why are you pretending? You are not asleep! Who was it got in at your window just now?"

"Mm . . . m . . . good morning! Got in at the window? Who could get in?"

"Oh come, it's no use your trying to keep it up! You'd better tell your scamp to clear out while he can! Do you hear? He's no business to be here!"

"Are you out of your senses, sir, bless you? Do you think I'd be such a fool? Here one's running about all day long, never a minute to sit down and then spoken to like this at night! Four roubles a month . . . and to find my own tea and sugar and this is all the credit I get for it! I used to live in a tradesman's house, and never met with such insult there!"

"Come, come - no need to go over your grievances! This very minute your grenadier must turn out! Do you understand?"

"You ought to be ashamed, sir," said Pelagea, and he could hear the tears in her voice. "Gentlefolks . . . educated, and yet not a notion that with our hard lot . . . in our life of toil" - she burst into tears. "It's easy to insult us. There's no one to stand up for us."

"Come, come . . . I don't mind! Your mistress sent me. You may let a devil in at the window for all I care!"

There was nothing left for the assistant procurator but

to acknowledge himself in the wrong and go back to his spouse.

"I say, Pelagea," he said, "you had my dressing-gown to brush. Where is it?"

"Oh, I am so sorry, sir; I forgot to put it on your chair. It's hanging on a peg near the stove."

Gagin felt for the dressing-gown by the stove, put it on, and went quietly back to his room.

When her husband went out Marya Mihalovna got into bed and waited. For the first three minutes her mind was at rest, but after that she began to feel uneasy.

"What a long time he's gone," she thought. "It's all right if he is there . . . that immoral man . . . but if it's a burglar?"

And again her imagination drew a picture of her husband going into the dark kitchen . . . a blow with an axe . . . dying without uttering a single sound . . . a pool of blood! . . .

Five minutes passed . . . five and a half . . . at last six. . . .

A cold sweat came out on her forehead.

"*Basile!*" she shrieked, "*Basile!*"

"What are you shouting for? I am here." She heard her husband's voice and steps. "Are you being murdered?"

The assistant procurator went up to the bedstead and sat down on the edge of it.

"There's nobody there at all," he said. "It was your fancy, you queer creature. . . . You can sleep easy, your fool of a Pelagea is as virtuous as her mistress. What a coward you are! What a . . . ."

And the deputy procurator began teasing his wife. He was wide awake now and did not want to go to sleep again.

"You are a coward!" he laughed. "You'd better go to the doctor to-morrow and tell him about your hallucinations. You are a neurotic!"

"What a smell of tar," said his wife - "tar or something . . . onion . . . cabbage soup!"

"Y-yes! There is a smell . . . I am not sleepy. I say, I'll light the candle. . . . Where are the matches? And, by the way, I'll show you the photograph of the procurator of the Palace of Justice. He gave us all a photograph when he said good-bye to us yesterday, with his autograph."

Gagin struck a match against the wall and lighted a candle. But before he had moved a step from the bed to fetch the photographs he heard behind him a piercing, heartrending shriek. Looking round, he saw his wife's large eyes fastened upon him, full of amazement, horror, and wrath. . . .

"You took your dressing-gown off in the kitchen?" she said, turning pale.

"Why?"

"Look at yourself!"

The deputy procurator looked down at himself, and gasped.

Flung over his shoulders was not his dressing-gown, but the fireman's overcoat. How had it come on his shoulders? While he was settling that question, his wife's imagination was drawing another picture, awful and impossible: darkness, stillness, whispering, and so on, and so on.

A PLAY

"PAVEL VASSILYEVITCH, there's a lady here, asking for you," Luka announced. "She's been waiting a good hour. . . ."

Pavel Vassilyevitch had only just finished lunch. Hearing of the lady, he frowned and said:

"Oh, damn her! Tell her I'm busy."

"She has been here five times already, Pavel Vassilyevitch. She says she really must see you. . . . She's almost crying."

"H'm . . . very well, then, ask her into the study."

Without haste Pavel Vassilyevitch put on his coat, took a pen in one hand, and a book in the other, and trying to look as though he were very busy he went into the study. There the visitor was awaiting him - a large stout lady with a red, beefy face, in spectacles. She looked very respectable, and her dress was more than fashionable (she had on a crinolette of four storeys and a high hat with a reddish bird in it). On seeing him she turned up her eyes and folded her hands in supplication.

"You don't remember me, of course," she began in a

high masculine tenor, visibly agitated. "I . . . I have had the pleasure of meeting you at the Hrutskys. . . . I am Mme. Murashkin. . . ."

"A. . . a . . . a . . . h'm . . . Sit down! What can I do for you?"

"You . . . you see . . . I . . . I . . ." the lady went on, sitting down and becoming still more agitated. "You don't remember me. . . . I'm Mme. Murashkin. . . . You see I'm a great admirer of your talent and always read your articles with great enjoyment. . . . Don't imagine I'm flattering you - God forbid! - I'm only giving honour where honour is due. . . . I am always reading you . . . always! To some extent I am myself not a stranger to literature - that is, of course . . . I will not venture to call myself an authoress, but . . . still I have added my little quota . . . I have published at different times three stories for children. . . . You have not read them, of course. . . . I have translated a good deal and . . . and my late brother used to write for *The Cause*."

"To be sure . . . er - er - er - What can I do for you?"

"You see . . . (the lady cast down her eyes and turned redder) I know your talents . . . your views, Pavel Vassilyevitch, and I have been longing to learn your opinion, or more exactly . . . to ask your advice. I must tell you I have perpetrated a play, my first-born - *pardon pour l'expression!* - and before sending it to the Censor I should like above all things to have your opinion on it."

Nervously, with the flutter of a captured bird, the lady fumbled in her skirt and drew out a fat manuscript.

Pavel Vassilyevitch liked no articles but his own. When threatened with the necessity of reading other people's, or listening to them, he felt as though he were facing the cannon's mouth. Seeing the manuscript he took fright and hastened to say:

"Very good, . . . leave it, . . . I'll read it."

"Pavel Vassilyevitch," the lady said languishingly, clasping her hands and raising them in supplication, "I know you're busy. . . . Your every minute is precious, and I know you're inwardly cursing me at this moment, but . . . Be kind, allow me to read you my play . . . . Do be so very sweet!"

"I should be delighted . . ." faltered Pavel Vassilyevitch; "but, Madam, I'm . . . I'm very busy . . . . I'm . . . I'm obliged to set off this minute."

"Pavel Vassilyevitch," moaned the lady and her eyes filled with tears, "I'm asking a sacrifice! I am insolent, I am intrusive, but be magnanimous. To-morrow I'm leaving for Kazan and I should like to know your opinion to-day. Grant me half an hour of your attention . . . only one half-hour . . . I implore you!"

Pavel Vassilyevitch was cotton-wool at core, and could not refuse. When it seemed to him that the lady was about to burst into sobs and fall on her knees, he was overcome with confusion and muttered helplessly.

"Very well; certainly . . . I will listen . . . I will give you half an hour."

The lady uttered a shriek of joy, took off her hat and settling herself, began to read. At first she read a scene in which a footman and a house maid, tidying up a sumptuous drawing-room, talked at length about their young lady, Anna Sergyevna, who was building a school and a hospital in the village. When the footman had left the room, the maidservant pronounced a monologue to the effect that education is light and ignorance is darkness; then Mme. Murashkin brought the footman back into the drawing-room and set him uttering a long monologue concerning his master, the General, who disliked his daughter's views, intended to marry her to a rich *kammer junker*, and held that the salvation of the people lay in unadulterated ignorance. Then, when the servants had left the stage, the young lady herself appeared and informed the audience that she had not slept all night, but had been thinking of Valentin Ivanovitch, who was the son of a poor teacher and assisted his sick father gratuitously. Valentin had studied all the sciences, but had no faith in friendship nor in love; he had no object in life and longed for death, and therefore she, the young lady, must save him.

Pavel Vassilyevitch listened, and thought with yearning anguish of his sofa. He scanned the lady viciously, felt her masculine tenor thumping on his eardrums, understood nothing, and thought:

"The devil sent you . . . as though I wanted to listen to your tosh! It's not my fault you've written a play, is it? My God! what a thick manuscript! What an infliction!"

Pavel Vassilyevitch glanced at the wall where the portrait of his wife was hanging and remembered that his wife had asked him to buy and bring to their summer cottage five yards of tape, a pound of cheese, and some tooth-powder.

"I hope I've not lost the pattern of that tape," he thought, "where did I put it? I believe it's in my blue reefer jacket. . . . Those wretched flies have covered her portrait with spots already, I must tell Olga to wash the glass. . . . She's reading the twelfth scene, so we must soon be at the end of the first act. As though inspiration were possible in this heat and with such a mountain of flesh, too! Instead of writing plays she'd much better eat cold vinegar hash and sleep in a cellar. . . ."

"You don't think that monologue's a little too long?" the lady asked suddenly, raising her eyes.

Pavel Vassilyevitch had not heard the monologue, and said in a voice as guilty as though not the lady but he had written that monologue:

"No, no, not at all. It's very nice. . . ."

The lady beamed with happiness and continued reading:

ANNA: You are consumed by analysis. Too early you have ceased to live in the heart and have put your faith in the intellect.

VALENTIN: What do you mean by the heart? That is a concept of anatomy. As a conventional term for what are called the feelings, I do not admit it.

ANNA *(confused)*: And love? Surely that is not merely a product of the association of ideas? Tell me frankly, have you ever loved?

VALENTIN *(bitterly)*: Let us not touch on old wounds

not yet healed. *(A pause.)* What are you thinking of?

ANNA: I believe you are unhappy.

During the sixteenth scene Pavel Vassilyevitch yawned, and accidently made with his teeth the sound dogs make when they catch a fly. He was dismayed at this unseemly sound, and to cover it assumed an expression of rapt attention.

"Scene seventeen! When will it end?" he thought. "Oh, my God! If this torture is prolonged another ten minutes I shall shout for the police. It's insufferable."

But at last the lady began reading more loudly and more rapidly, and finally raising her voice she read *"Curtain."*

Pavel Vassilyevitch uttered a faint sigh and was about to get up, but the lady promptly turned the page and went on reading.

ACT II. - *Scene, a village street. On right, School. On left, Hospital.* Villagers, *male and female, sitting on the hospital steps.*

"Excuse me," Pavel Vassilyevitch broke in, "how many acts are there?"

"Five," answered the lady, and at once, as though fearing her audience might escape her, she went on rapidly.

VALENTIN *is looking out of the schoolhouse window. In the background* Villagers *can be seen taking their goods to the Inn.*

Like a man condemned to be executed and convinced of the impossibility of a reprieve, Pavel Vassilyevitch gave up expecting the end, abandoned all hope, and simply tried to prevent his eyes from closing, and to retain an expression of attention on his face. . . . The future when the lady would finish her play and depart seemed to him so remote that he did not even think of it.

"Trooo - too - too - too . . ." the lady's voice sounded in his ears. "Troo - too - too . . . sh - sh - sh - sh . . ."

"I forgot to take my soda," he thought. "What am I thinking about? Oh - my soda. . . . Most likely I shall have a bilious attack. . . . It's extraordinary, Smirnovsky swills vodka all day long and yet he never has a bilious attack. . . . There's a bird settled on the window . . . a sparrow. . . ."

Pavel Vassilyevitch made an effort to unglue his strained and closing eyelids, yawned without opening his mouth, and stared at Mme. Murashkin. She grew misty and swayed before his eyes, turned into a triangle and her head pressed against the ceiling. . . .

VALENTIN No, let me depart.

ANNA *(in dismay)*: Why?

VALENTIN *(aside)*: She has turned pale! *(To her)* Do not force me to explain. Sooner would I die than you should know the reason.

ANNA *(after a pause)*: You cannot go away. . . .

The lady began to swell, swelled to an immense size,

and melted into the dingy atmosphere of the study - only her moving mouth was visible; then she suddenly dwindled to the size of a bottle, swayed from side to side, and with the table retreated to the further end of the room . . .

VALENTIN *(holding ANNA in his arms)*: You have given me new life! You have shown me an object to live for! You have renewed me as the Spring rain renews the awakened earth! But . . . it is too late, too late! The ill that gnaws at my heart is beyond cure. . . .

Pavel Vassilyevitch started and with dim and smarting eyes stared at the reading lady; for a minute he gazed fixedly as though understanding nothing. . . .

SCENE XI. - *The same. The* BARON *and the* POLICE INSPECTOR *with assistants.*

VALENTIN: Take me!

ANNA: I am his! Take me too! Yes, take me too! I love him, I love him more than life!

BARON: Anna Sergyevna, you forget that you are ruining your father . . . .

The lady began swelling again. . . . Looking round him wildly Pavel Vassilyevitch got up, yelled in a deep, unnatural voice, snatched from the table a heavy paper-weight, and beside himself, brought it down with all his force on the authoress's head. . . .

* * * * *

"Give me in charge, I've killed her!" he said to the

maidservant who ran in, a minute later.

The jury acquitted him.

A MYSTERY

ON the evening of Easter Sunday the actual Civil Councillor, Navagin, on his return from paying calls, picked up the sheet of paper on which visitors had inscribed their names in the hall, and went with it into his study. After taking off his outer garments and drinking some seltzer water, he settled himself comfortably on a couch and began reading the signatures in the list. When his eyes reached the middle of the long list of signatures, he started, gave an ejaculation of astonishment and snapped his fingers, while his face expressed the utmost perplexity.

"Again!" he said, slapping his knee. "It's extraordinary! Again! Again there is the signature of that fellow, goodness knows who he is! Fedyukov! Again!"

Among the numerous signatures on the paper was the signature of a certain Fedyukov. Who the devil this Fedyukov was, Navagin had not a notion. He went over in his memory all his acquaintances, relations and subordinates in the service, recalled his remote past but could recollect no name like Fedyukov. What was so strange was that this *incognito*, Fedyukov, had signed his name regularly every Christmas and Easter for the last thirteen years. Neither Navagin, his wife, nor his house porter knew who he was, where he came from or what he was like.

"It's extraordinary!" Navagin thought in perplexity, as he paced about the study. "It's strange and incomprehensible! It's like sorcery!"

"Call the porter here!" he shouted.

"It's devilish queer! But I will find out who he is!"

"I say, Grigory," he said, addressing the porter as he entered, "that Fedyukov has signed his name again! Did you see him?"

"No, your Excellency."

"Upon my word, but he has signed his name! So he must have been in the hall. Has he been?"

"No, he hasn't, your Excellency."

"How could he have signed his name without being there?"

"I can't tell."

"Who is to tell, then? You sit gaping there in the hall. Try and remember, perhaps someone you didn't know came in? Think a minute!"

"No, your Excellency, there has been no one I didn't know. Our clerks have been, the baroness came to see her Excellency, the priests have been with the Cross, and there has been no one else. . . ."

"Why, he was invisible when he signed his name, then, was he?"

Anton Chekhov

"I can't say: but there has been no Fedyukov here. That I will swear before the holy image. . . ."

"It's queer! It's incomprehensible! It's ex-traordinary!" mused Navagin. "It's positively ludicrous. A man has been signing his name here for thirteen years and you can't find out who he is. Perhaps it's a joke? Perhaps some clerk writes that name as well as his own for fun."

And Navagin began examining Fedyukov's signature.

The bold, florid signature in the old-fashioned style with twirls and flourishes was utterly unlike the handwriting of the other signatures. It was next below the signature of Shtutchkin, the provincial secretary, a scared, timorous little man who would certainly have died of fright if he had ventured upon such an impudent joke.

"The mysterious Fedyukov has signed his name again!" said Navagin, going in to see his wife. "Again I fail to find out who he is."

Madame Navagin was a spiritualist, and so for all phenomena in nature, comprehensible or incomprehensible, she had a very simple explanation.

"There's nothing extraordinary about it," she said. "You don't believe it, of course, but I have said it already and I say it again: there is a great deal in the world that is supernatural, which our feeble intellect can never grasp. I am convinced that this Fedyukov is a spirit who has a sympathy for you . . . If I were you, I would call him up and ask him what he wants."

"Nonsense, nonsense!"

Navagin was free from superstitions, but the phenomenon which interested him was so mysterious that all sorts of uncanny devilry intruded into his mind against his will. All the evening he was imagining that the incognito Fedyukov was the spirit of some long-dead clerk, who had been discharged from the service by Navagin's ancestors and was now revenging himself on their descendant; or perhaps it was the kinsman of some petty official dismissed by Navagin himself, or of a girl seduced by him. . . .

All night Navagin dreamed of a gaunt old clerk in a shabby uniform, with a face as yellow as a lemon, hair that stood up like a brush, and pewtery eyes; the clerk said something in a sepulchral voice and shook a bony finger at him. And Navagin almost had an attack of inflammation of the brain.

For a fortnight he was silent and gloomy and kept walking up and down and thinking. In the end he overcame his sceptical vanity, and going into his wife's room he said in a hollow voice:

"Zina, call up Fedyukov!"

The spiritualistic lady was delighted; she sent for a sheet of cardboard and a saucer, made her husband sit down beside her, and began upon the magic rites.

Fedyukov did not keep them waiting long. . . .

"What do you want?" asked Navagin.

"Repent," answered the saucer.

"What were you on earth?"

"A sinner. . . ."

"There, you see!" whispered his wife, "and you did not believe!"

Navagin conversed for a long time with Fedyukov, and then called up Napoleon, Hannibal, Askotchensky, his aunt Klavdya Zaharovna, and they all gave him brief but correct answers full of deep significance. He was busy with the saucer for four hours, and fell asleep soothed and happy that he had become acquainted with a mysterious world that was new to him. After that he studied spiritualism every day, and at the office, informed the clerks that there was a great deal in nature that was supernatural and marvellous to which our men of science ought to have turned their attention long ago.

Hypnotism, mediumism, bishopism, spiritualism, the fourth dimension, and other misty notions took complete possession of him, so that for whole days at a time, to the great delight of his wife, he read books on spiritualism or devoted himself to the saucer, table-turning, and discussions of supernatural phenomena. At his instigation all his clerks took up spiritualism, too, and with such ardour that the old managing clerk went out of his mind and one day sent a telegram: "Hell. Government House. I feel that I am turning into an evil spirit. What's to be done? Reply paid. Vassily Krinolinsky."

After reading several hundreds of treatises on spiritualism Navagin had a strong desire to write something himself. For five months he sat composing, and in the end had written a huge monograph, entitled: *My Opinion*. When he had finished this essay he determined to send it to a spiritualist journal.

The day on which it was intended to despatch it to the journal was a very memorable one for him. Navagin remembers that on that never-to-be-forgotten day the secretary who had made a fair copy of his article and the sacristan of the parish who had been sent for on business were in his study. Nayagin's face was beaming. He looked lovingly at his creation, felt between his fingers how thick it was, and with a happy smile said to the secretary:

"I propose, Filipp Sergeyitch, to send it registered. It will be safer. . . ." And raising his eyes to the sacristan, he said: "I have sent for you on business, my good man. I am putting my youngest son to the high school and I must have a certificate of baptism; only could you let me have it quickly?"

"Very good, your Excellency!" said the sacristan, bowing. "Very good, I understand. . . ."

"Can you let me have it by to-morrow?"

"Very well, your Excellency, set your mind at rest! To-morrow it shall be ready! Will you send someone to the church to-morrow before evening service? I shall be there. Bid him ask for Fedyukov. I am always there. . . ."

"What!" cried the general, turning pale.

"Fedyukov."

"You, . . . you are Fedyukov?" asked Navagin, looking at him with wide-open eyes.

"Just so, Fedyukov."

"You. . . . you signed your name in my hall?"

"Yes . . ." the sacristan admitted, and was overcome with confusion. "When we come with the Cross, your Excellency, to grand gentlemen's houses I always sign my name. . . . I like doing it. . . . Excuse me, but when I see the list of names in the hall I feel an impulse to sign mine. . . ."

In dumb stupefaction, understanding nothing, hearing nothing, Navagin paced about his study. He touched the curtain over the door, three times waved his hands like a *jeune premier* in a ballet when he sees *her*, gave a whistle and a meaningless smile, and pointed with his finger into space.

"So I will send off the article at once, your Excellency," said the secretary.

These words roused Navagin from his stupour. He looked blankly at the secretary and the sacristan, remembered, and stamping, his foot irritably, screamed in a high, breaking tenor:

"Leave me in peace! Lea-eave me in peace, I tell you! What you want of me I don't understand."

The secretary and the sacristan went out of the study and reached the street while he was still stamping and shouting:

"Leave me in peace! What you want of me I don't understand. Lea-eave me in peace!"

Anton Chekhov

STRONG IMPRESSIONS

IT happened not so long ago in the Moscow circuit court. The jurymen, left in the court for the night, before lying down to sleep fell into conversation about strong impressions. They were led to this discussion by recalling a witness who, by his own account, had begun to stammer and had gone grey owing to a terrible moment. The jurymen decided that before going to sleep, each one of them should ransack among his memories and tell something that had happened to him. Man's life is brief, but yet there is no man who cannot boast that there have been terrible moments in his past.

One juryman told the story of how he was nearly drowned; another described how, in a place where there were neither doctors nor chemists, he had one night poisoned his own son through giving him zinc vitriol by mistake for soda. The child did not die, but the father nearly went out of his mind. A third, a man not old but in bad health, told how he had twice attempted to commit suicide: the first time by shooting himself and the second time by throwing himself before a train.

The fourth, a foppishly dressed, fat little man, told us the following story:

"I was not more than twenty-two or twenty-three when I fell head over ears in love with my present wife and made her an offer. Now I could with pleasure thrash myself for my early marriage, but at the time, I don't know what would have become of me if Natasha had refused me. My love was absolutely the real thing, just as it is described in novels - frantic, passionate, and so on. My happiness overwhelmed me and I did not know how to get away from it, and I bored my father and my friends and the servants, continually talking about the fervour of my passion. Happy people are the most sickening bores. I was a fearful bore; I feel ashamed of it even now. . . .

"Among my friends there was in those days a young man who was beginning his career as a lawyer. Now he is a lawyer known all over Russia; in those days he was only just beginning to gain recognition and was not rich and famous enough to be entitled to cut an old friend when he met him. I used to go and see him once or twice a week. We used to loll on sofas and begin discussing philosophy.

"One day I was lying on his sofa, arguing that there was no more ungrateful profession than that of a lawyer. I tried to prove that as soon as the examination of witnesses is over the court can easily dispense with both the counsels for the prosecution and for the defence, because they are neither of them necessary and are only in the way. If a grown-up juryman, morally and mentally sane, is convinced that the ceiling is white, or that Ivanov is guilty, to struggle with that conviction and to vanquish it is beyond the power of any Demosthenes. Who can convince me that I have a red moustache when I know that it is black? As I listen to an orator I may perhaps grow sentimental and weep, but my fundamental conviction, based for the most part on unmistakable evidence and fact, is not changed in the least. My lawyer maintained that I was young and foolish and that I was talking childish nonsense. In his opinion, for one thing, an obvious fact becomes still more obvious through light being thrown upon it by conscientious, well-informed people; for another, talent is an elemental force, a hurricane capable of turning even stones to dust, let alone such trifles as the convictions of artisans and merchants of the second guild. It is as hard for human weakness to struggle against talent as to look at the sun without winking, or to stop the wind. One simple mortal by the power of the word turns thousands of convinced savages to Christianity; Odysseus was a man of the firmest convictions, but he succumbed to the Syrens, and so on. All history consists of similar examples, and in life they are met with at every turn; and so it is bound to be, or the intelligent and talented man would have no superiority over the stupid and incompetent.

"I stuck to my point, and went on maintaining that convictions are stronger than any talent, though, frankly speaking, I could not have defined exactly what I meant by conviction or what I meant by talent. Most likely I simply talked for the sake of talking.

"'Take you, for example,' said the lawyer. 'You are convinced at this moment that your fiancee is an angel and that there is not a man in the whole town happier than you. But I tell you: ten or twenty minutes would be enough for me to make you sit down to this table and write to your fiancee, breaking off your engagement.

"I laughed.

"'Don't laugh, I am speaking seriously,' said my friend. 'If I choose, in twenty minutes you will be happy at the thought that you need not get married. Goodness knows what talent I have, but you are not one of the strong sort.'

"'Well, try it on!' said I.

"'No, what for? I am only telling you this. You are a good boy and it would be cruel to subject you to such an experiment. And besides I am not in good form to-day.'

"We sat down to supper. The wine and the thought of Natasha, my beloved, flooded my whole being with youth and happiness. My happiness was so boundless that the lawyer sitting opposite to me with his green eyes seemed to me an unhappy man, so small, so grey. . . .

"'Do try!' I persisted. 'Come, I entreat you!'

"The lawyer shook his head and frowned. Evidently I was beginning to bore him.

"'I know,' he said, 'after my experiment you will say, thank you, and will call me your saviour; but you see I must think of your fiancee too. She loves you; your jilting her would make her suffer. And what a charming creature she is! I envy you.'

"The lawyer sighed, sipped his wine, and began talking of how charming my Natasha was. He had an extra-ordinary gift of description. He could knock you off a regular string of words about a woman's eyelashes or her little finger. I listened to him with relish.

"'I have seen a great many women in my day,' he said, 'but I give you my word of honour, I speak as a friend, your Natasha Andreyevna is a pearl, a rare girl. Of course she has her defects - many of them, in fact, if you like - but still she is fascinating.'

"And the lawyer began talking of my fiancee's defects. Now I understand very well that he was talking of women in general, of their weak points in general, but at the time it seemed to me that he was talking only of Natasha. He went into ecstasies over her turn-up nose, her shrieks, her shrill laugh, her airs and graces, precisely all the things I so disliked in her. All that was, to his thinking, infinitely sweet, graceful, and feminine.

"Without my noticing it, he quickly passed from his enthusiastic tone to one of fatherly admonition, and then to a light and derisive one. . . . There was no presiding judge and no one to check the diffusiveness of the lawyer. I had not time to open my mouth, besides, what could I say? What my friend said was not new, it was what everyone has known for ages, and the whole venom lay not in what he said, but in the damnable form he put it in. It really was beyond anything!

"As I listened to him then I learned that the same word has thousands of shades of meaning according to the tone in which it is pronounced, and the form which is given to the sentence. Of course I cannot reproduce the tone or the form; I can only say that as I listened to my friend and walked up and down the room, I was moved to resentment, indignation, and contempt together with him. I even believed him when with tears in his eyes he informed me that I was a great man, that I was worthy of a better fate, that I was destined to achieve something in the future which marriage would hinder!

"'My friend!' he exclaimed, pressing my hand. 'I beseech you, I adjure you: stop before it is too late. Stop! May Heaven preserve you from this strange, cruel mistake! My friend, do not ruin your youth!'

"Believe me or not, as you choose, but the long and the short of it was that I sat down to the table and wrote to my fiancee, breaking off the engagement. As I wrote I felt relieved that it was not yet too late to rectify my mistake. Sealing the letter, I hastened out into the street to post it. The lawyer himself came with me.

"'Excellent! Capital!' he applauded me as my letter to Natasha disappeared into the darkness of the box. 'I congratulate you with all my heart. I am glad for you.'

"After walking a dozen paces with me the lawyer went on:

"'Of course, marriage has its good points. I, for instance, belong to the class of people to whom marriage and home life is everything.'

"And he proceeded to describe his life, and lay before me all the hideousness of a solitary bachelor existence.

"He spoke with enthusiasm of his future wife, of the sweets of ordinary family life, and was so eloquent, so sincere in his ecstasies that by the time we had reached his door, I was in despair.

"'What are you doing to me, you horrible man?' I said, gasping. 'You have ruined me! Why did you make me write that cursed letter? I love her, I love her!'

"And I protested my love. I was horrified at my conduct which now seemed to me wild and senseless. It is impossible, gentlemen, to imagine a more violent emotion than I experienced at that moment. Oh, what I went through, what I suffered! If some kind person had thrust a revolver into my hand at that moment, I should have put a bullet through my brains with pleasure.

"'Come, come . . .' said the lawyer, slapping me on the shoulder, and he laughed. 'Give over crying. The letter won't reach your fiancee. It was not you who wrote the address but I, and I muddled it so they won't be able to make it out at the post-office. It will be a lesson to you not to argue about what you don't understand.'

"Now, gentlemen, I leave it to the next to speak."

The fifth juryman settled himself more comfortably, and had just opened his mouth to begin his story when we heard the clock strike on Spassky Tower.

"Twelve . . ." one of the jurymen counted. "And into which class, gentlemen, would you put the emotions that are being experienced now by the man we are trying? He, that murderer, is spending the night in a convict cell here in the court, sitting or lying down and of course not sleeping, and throughout the whole sleepless night listening to that chime. What is he thinking of? What visions are haunting him?"

And the jurymen all suddenly forgot about strong impressions; what their companion who had once written a letter to his Natasha had suffered seemed unimportant, even not amusing; and no one said anything more; they began quietly and in silence lying down to sleep.

Anton Chekhov

DRUNK

A MANUFACTURER called Frolov, a handsome dark man with a round beard, and a soft, velvety expression in his eyes, and Almer, his lawyer, an elderly man with a big rough head, were drinking in one of the public rooms of a restaurant on the outskirts of the town. They had both come to the restaurant straight from a ball and so were wearing dress coats and white ties. Except them and the waiters at the door there was not a soul in the room; by Frolov's orders no one else was admitted.

They began by drinking a big wine-glass of vodka and eating oysters.

"Good!" said Almer. "It was I brought oysters into fashion for the first course, my boy. The vodka burns and stings your throat and you have a voluptuous sensation in your throat when you swallow an oyster. Don't you?"

A dignified waiter with a shaven upper lip and grey whiskers put a sauceboat on the table.

"What's that you are serving?" asked Frolov.

"Sauce Provencale for the herring, sir. . . ."

"What! is that the way to serve it?" shouted Frolov, not looking into the sauceboat. "Do you call that sauce? You don't know how to wait, you blockhead!"

Frolov's velvety eyes flashed. He twisted a corner of the table-cloth round his finger, made a slight movement, and the dishes, the candlesticks, and the bottles, all jingling and clattering, fell with a crash on the floor.

The waiters, long accustomed to pot-house catastrophes, ran up to the table and began picking up the fragments with grave and unconcerned faces, like surgeons at an operation.

"How well you know how to manage them!" said Almer, and he laughed. "But . . . move a little away from the table or you will step in the caviare."

"Call the engineer here!" cried Frolov.

This was the name given to a decrepit, doleful old man who really had once been an engineer and very well off; he had squandered all his property and towards the end of his life had got into a restaurant where he looked after the waiters and singers and carried out various commissions relating to the fair sex. Appearing at the summons, he put his head on one side respectfully.

"Listen, my good man," Frolov said, addressing him. "What's the meaning of this disorder? How queerly you fellows wait! Don't you know that I don't like it? Devil take you, I shall give up coming to you!"

"I beg you graciously to excuse it, Alexey

Semyonitch!" said the engineer, laying his hand on his heart. "I will take steps immediately, and your slightest wishes shall be carried out in the best and speediest way."

"Well, that'll do, you can go. . . ."

The engineer bowed, staggered back, still doubled up, and disappeared through the doorway with a final flash of the false diamonds on his shirt-front and fingers.

The table was laid again. Almer drank red wine and ate with relish some sort of bird served with truffles, and ordered a matelote of eelpouts and a sterlet with its tail in its mouth. Frolov only drank vodka and ate nothing but bread. He rubbed his face with his open hands, scowled, and was evidently out of humour. Both were silent. There was a stillness. Two electric lights in opaque shades flickered and hissed as though they were angry. The gypsy girls passed the door, softly humming.

"One drinks and is none the merrier," said Frolov. "The more I pour into myself, the more sober I become. Other people grow festive with vodka, but I suffer from anger, disgusting thoughts, sleeplessness. Why is it, old man, that people don't invent some other pleasure besides drunkenness and debauchery? It's really horrible!"

"You had better send for the gypsy girls."

"Confound them!"

The head of an old gypsy woman appeared in the door from the passage.

"Alexey Semyonitch, the gypsies are asking for tea and brandy," said the old woman. "May we order it?"

"Yes," answered Frolov. "You know they get a percentage from the restaurant keeper for asking the visitors to treat them. Nowadays you can't even believe a man when he asks for vodka. The people are all mean, vile, spoilt. Take these waiters, for instance. They have countenances like professors, and grey heads; they get two hundred roubles a month, they live in houses of their own and send their girls to the high school, but you may swear at them and give yourself airs as much as you please. For a rouble the engineer will gulp down a whole pot of mustard and crow like a cock. On my honour, if one of them would take offence I would make him a present of a thousand roubles."

"What's the matter with you?" said Almer, looking at him with surprise. "Whence this melancholy? You are red in the face, you look like a wild animal. . . . What's the matter with you?"

"It's horrid. There's one thing I can't get out of my head. It seems as though it is nailed there and it won't come out."

A round little old man, buried in fat and completely bald, wearing a short reefer jacket and lilac waistcoat and carrying a guitar, walked into the room. He made an idiotic face, drew himself up, and saluted like a soldier.

"Ah, the parasite!" said Frolov, "let me introduce him, he has made his fortune by grunting like a pig. Come here!" He poured vodka, wine, and brandy into a glass, sprinkled pepper and salt into it, mixed it all up and gave it to the parasite. The latter tossed it off and smacked his lips with gusto.

"He's accustomed to drink a mess so that pure wine makes him sick," said Frolov. "Come, parasite, sit down and sing."

The old man sat down, touched the strings with his fat fingers, and began singing:

"Neetka, neetka, Margareetka. . . ."

After drinking champagne Frolov was drunk. He thumped with his fist on the table and said:

"Yes, there's something that sticks in my head! It won't give me a minute's peace!"

"Why, what is it?"

"I can't tell you. It's a secret. It's something so private that I could only speak of it in my prayers. But if you like . . . as a sign of friendship, between ourselves . . . only mind, to no one, no, no, no, . . . I'll tell you, it will ease my heart, but for God's sake . . . listen and forget it. . . ."

Frolov bent down to Almer and for a minute breathed in his ear.

"I hate my wife!" he brought out.

The lawyer looked at him with surprise.

"Yes, yes, my wife, Marya Mihalovna," Frolov

muttered, flushing red. "I hate her and that's all about it."

"What for?"

"I don't know myself! I've only been married two years. I married as you know for love, and now I hate her like a mortal enemy, like this parasite here, saving your presence. And there is no cause, no sort of cause! When she sits by me, eats, or says anything, my whole soul boils, I can scarcely restrain myself from being rude to her. It's something one can't describe. To leave her or tell her the truth is utterly impossible because it would be a scandal, and living with her is worse than hell for me. I can't stay at home! I spend my days at business and in the restaurants and spend my nights in dissipation. Come, how is one to explain this hatred? She is not an ordinary woman, but handsome, clever, quiet."

The old man stamped his foot and began singing:

"I went a walk with a captain bold, And in his ear my secrets told."

"I must own I always thought that Marya Mihalovna was not at all the right person for you," said Almer after a brief silence, and he heaved a sigh.

"Do you mean she is too well educated? . . . I took the gold medal at the commercial school myself, I have been to Paris three times. I am not cleverer than you, of course, but I am no more foolish than my wife. No, brother, education is not the sore point. Let me tell you how all the trouble began. It began with my suddenly fancying that she had married me not from love, but for the sake of my money. This idea took possession of my brain. I have done all I could think of, but the cursed thing sticks! And to make it worse my wife was overtaken with a passion for luxury. Getting into a sack of gold after poverty, she took to flinging it in all directions. She went quite off her head, and was so carried away that she used to get through twenty thousand every month. And I am a distrustful man. I don't believe in anyone, I suspect everybody. And the more friendly you are to me the greater my torment. I keep fancying I am being flattered for my money. I trust no one! I am a difficult man, my boy, very difficult!"

Frolov emptied his glass at one gulp and went on.

"But that's all nonsense," he said. "One never ought to speak of it. It's stupid. I am tipsy and I have been chattering, and now you are looking at me with lawyer's eyes - glad you know some one else's secret. Well, well! . . . Let us drop this conversation. Let us drink! I say," he said, addressing a waiter, "is Mustafa here? Fetch him in!"

Shortly afterwards there walked into the room a little Tatar boy, aged about twelve, wearing a dress coat and white gloves.

"Come here!" Frolov said to him. "Explain to us the following fact: there was a time when you Tatars conquered us and took tribute from us, but now you serve us as waiters and sell dressing-gowns. How do you explain such a change?"

Mustafa raised his eyebrows and said in a shrill voice, with a sing-song intonation: "The mutability of destiny!"

Almer looked at his grave face and went off into peals of laughter.

"Well, give him a rouble!" said Frolov. "He is making his fortune out of the mutability of destiny. He is only kept here for the sake of those two words. Drink, Mustafa! You will make a gre-eat rascal! I mean it is awful how many of your sort are toadies hanging about rich men. The number of these peaceful bandits and robbers is beyond all reckoning! Shouldn't we send for the gypsies now? Eh? Fetch the gypsies along!"

The gypsies, who had been hanging about wearily in the corridors for a long time, burst with whoops into the room, and a wild orgy began.

"Drink!" Frolov shouted to them. "Drink! Seed of Pharaoh! Sing! A-a-ah!"

"In the winter time . . . o-o-ho! . . . the sledge was flying . . ."

The gypsies sang, whistled, danced. In the frenzy which sometimes takes possession of spoilt and very wealthy men, "broad natures," Frolov began to play the fool. He ordered supper and champagne for the gypsies, broke the shade of the electric light, shied bottles at the pictures and looking-glasses, and did it all apparently without the slightest enjoyment, scowling and shouting irritably, with contempt for the people, with an expression of hatred in his eyes and his manners. He made the engineer sing a solo, made the bass singers drink a mixture of wine, vodka, and oil.

At six o'clock they handed him the bill.

"Nine hundred and twenty-five roubles, forty kopecks," said Almer, and shrugged his shoulders. "What's it for? No, wait, we must go into it!"

"Stop!" muttered Frolov, pulling out his pocket-book. "Well! . . . let them rob me. That's what I'm rich for, to be robbed! . . . You can't get on without parasites! . . . You are my lawyer. You get six thousand a year out of me and what for? But excuse me, . . . I don't know what I am saying."

As he was returning home with Almer, Frolov murmured:

"Going home is awful to me! Yes! . . . There isn't a human being I can open my soul to. . . . They are all robbers . . . traitors . . . . Oh, why did I tell you my secret? Yes . . . why? Tell me why?"

At the entrance to his house, he craned forward towards Almer and, staggering, kissed him on the lips, having the old Moscow habit of kissing indiscriminately on every occasion.

"Good-bye . . . I am a difficult, hateful man," he said. "A horrid, drunken, shameless life. You are a well-educated, clever man, but you only laugh and drink with me . . . there's no help from any of you. . . . But if you were a friend to me, if you were an honest man, in reality you ought to have said to me: 'Ugh, you vile, hateful man! You reptile!'"

"Come, come," Almer muttered, "go to bed."

"There is no help from you; the only hope is that, when I am in the country in the summer, I may go out into the fields and a storm come on and the thunder may strike me dead on the spot. . . . Good-bye."

Frolov kissed Almer once more and muttering and dropping asleep as he walked, began mounting the stairs, supported by two footmen.

THE MARSHAL'S WIDOW

ON the first of February every year, St. Trifon's day, there is an extraordinary commotion on the estate of Madame Zavzyatov, the widow of Trifon Lvovitch, the late marshal of the district. On that day, the nameday of the deceased marshal, the widow Lyubov Petrovna has a requiem service celebrated in his memory, and after the requiem a thanksgiving to the Lord. The whole district assembles for the service. There you will see Hrumov the present marshal, Marfutkin, the president of the Zemstvo, Potrashkov, the permanent member of the Rural Board, the two justices of the peace of the district, the police captain, Krinolinov, two police-superintendents, the district doctor, Dvornyagin, smelling of iodoform, all the landowners, great and small, and so on. There are about fifty people assembled in all.

Precisely at twelve o'clock, the visitors, with long faces, make their way from all the rooms to the big hall. There are carpets on the floor and their steps are noiseless, but the solemnity of the occasion makes them instinctively walk on tip-toe, holding out their hands to balance themselves. In the hall everything is already prepared. Father Yevmeny, a little old man in a high faded cap, puts on his black vestments. Konkordiev, the deacon, already in his vestments, and as red as a crab, is noiselessly turning over the leaves of his missal and putting slips of paper in it. At the door leading to the vestibule, Luka, the sacristan, puffing out his cheeks and making round eyes, blows up the censer. The hall is gradually filled with bluish transparent smoke and the smell of incense.

Gelikonsky, the elementary schoolmaster, a young man with big pimples on his frightened face, wearing a new greatcoat like a sack, carries round wax candles on a silver-plated tray. The hostess, Lyubov Petrovna, stands in the front by a little table with a dish of funeral rice on it, and holds her handkerchief in readiness to her face. There is a profound stillness, broken from time to time by sighs. Everybody has a long, solemn face. . . .

The requiem service begins. The blue smoke curls up from the censer and plays in the slanting sunbeams, the lighted candles faintly splutter. The singing, at first harsh and deafening, soon becomes quiet and musical as the choir gradually adapt themselves to the acoustic conditions of the rooms. . . . The tunes are all mournful and sad. . . . The guests are gradually brought to a melancholy mood and grow pensive. Thoughts of the brevity of human life, of mutability, of worldly vanity stray through their brains. . . . They recall the deceased Zavzyatov, a thick-set, red-cheeked man who used to drink off a bottle of champagne at one gulp and smash looking-glasses with his forehead. And when they sing "With Thy Saints, O Lord," and the sobs of their hostess are audible, the guests shift uneasily from one foot to the other. The more emotional begin to feel a tickling in their throat and about their eyelids. Marfutkin, the president of the Zemstvo, to stifle the unpleasant feeling, bends down to the police captain's ear and whispers:

Anton Chekhov

"I was at Ivan Fyodoritch's yesterday. . . . . Pyotr Petrovitch and I took all the tricks, playing no trumps . . . . Yes, indeed. . . . Olga Andreyevna was so exasperated that her false tooth fell out of her mouth."

But at last the "Eternal Memory" is sung. Gelikonsky respectfully takes away the candles, and the memorial service is over. Thereupon there follows a momentary commotion; there is a changing of vestments and a thanksgiving service. After the thanksgiving, while Father Yevmeny is disrobing, the visitors rub their hands and cough, while their hostess tells some anecdote of the good-heartedness of the deceased Trifon Lvovitch.

"Pray come to lunch, friends," she says, concluding her story with a sigh.

The visitors, trying not to push or tread on each other's feet, hasten into the dining-room. . . . There the luncheon is awaiting them. The repast is so magnificent that the deacon Konkordiev thinks it his duty every year to fling up his hands as he looks at it and, shaking his head in amazement, say:

"Supernatural! It's not so much like human fare, Father Yevmeny, as offerings to the gods."

The lunch is certainly exceptional. Everything that the flora and fauna of the country can furnish is on the table, but the only thing supernatural about it, perhaps, is that on the table there is everything except . . . alcoholic beverages. Lyubov Petrovna has taken a vow never to have in her house cards or spirituous liquors - the two sources of her husband's ruin. And the only bottles contain oil and vinegar, as though in mockery and chastisement of the guests who are to a man desperately fond of the bottle, and given to tippling.

"Please help yourselves, gentlemen!" the marshal's widow presses them. "Only you must excuse me, I have no vodka. . . . I have none in the house."

The guests approach the table and hesitatingly attack the pie. But the progress with eating is slow. In the plying of forks, in the cutting up and munching, there is a certain sloth and apathy. . . . Evidently something is wanting.

"I feel as though I had lost something," one of the justices of the peace whispers to the other. "I feel as I did when my wife ran away with the engineer. . . . I can't eat."

Marfutkin, before beginning to eat, fumbles for a long time in his pocket and looks for his handkerchief.

"Oh, my handkerchief must be in my greatcoat," he recalls in a loud voice, "and here I am looking for it," and he goes into the vestibule where the fur coats are hanging up.

He returns from the vestibule with glistening eyes, and at once attacks the pie with relish.

"I say, it's horrid munching away with a dry mouth, isn't it?" he whispers to Father Yevmeny. "Go into the vestibule, Father. There's a bottle there in my fur coat. . . . Only mind you are careful; don't make a clatter with the bottle."

Father Yevmeny recollects that he has some direction

to give to Luka, and trips off to the vestibule.

"Father, a couple of words in confidence," says Dvornyagin, overtaking him.

"You should see the fur coat I've bought myself, gentlemen," Hrumov boasts. "It's worth a thousand, and I gave . . . you won't believe it . . . two hundred and fifty! Not a farthing more."

At any other time the guests would have greeted this information with indifference, but now they display surprise and incredulity. In the end they all troop out into the vestibule to look at the fur coat, and go on looking at it till the doctor's man Mikeshka carries five empty bottles out on the sly. When the steamed sturgeon is served, Marfutkin remembers that he has left his cigar case in his sledge and goes to the stable. That he may not be lonely on this expedition, he takes with him the deacon, who appropriately feels it necessary to have a look at his horse. . . .

On the evening of the same day, Lyubov Petrovna is sitting in her study, writing a letter to an old friend in Petersburg:

"To-day, as in past years," she writes among other things, "I had a memorial service for my dear husband. All my neighbours came to the service. They are a simple, rough set, but what hearts! I gave them a splendid lunch, but of course, as in previous years, without a drop of alcoholic liquor. Ever since he died from excessive drinking I have vowed to establish temperance in this district and thereby to expiate his sins. I have begun the campaign for temperance at my own house. Father Yevmeny is delighted with my efforts, and helps me both in word and deed. Oh, *ma chere*, if you knew how fond my bears are of me! The president of the Zemstvo, Marfutkin, kissed my hand after lunch, held it a long while to his lips, and, wagging his head in an absurd way, burst into tears: so much feeling but no words! Father Yevmeny, that delightful little old man, sat down by me, and looking tearfully at me kept babbling something like a child. I did not understand what he said, but I know how to understand true feeling. The police captain, the handsome man of whom I wrote to you, went down on his knees to me, tried to read me some verses of his own composition (he is a poet), but . . . his feelings were too much for him, he lurched and fell over . . . that huge giant went into hysterics, you can imagine my delight! The day did not pass without a hitch, however. Poor Alalykin, the president of the judges' assembly, a stout and apoplectic man, was overcome by illness and lay on the sofa in a state of unconsciousness for two hours. We had to pour water on him. . . . I am thankful to Doctor Dvornyagin: he had brought a bottle of brandy from his dispensary and he moistened the patient's temples, which quickly revived him, and he was able to be moved. . . ."

Anton Chekhov

A BAD BUSINESS

"WHO goes there?"

No answer. The watchman sees nothing, but through the roar of the wind and the trees distinctly hears someone walking along the avenue ahead of him. A March night, cloudy and foggy, envelopes the earth, and it seems to the watchman that the earth, the sky, and he himself with his thoughts are all merged together into something vast and impenetrably black. He can only grope his way.

"Who goes there?" the watchman repeats, and he begins to fancy that he hears whispering and smothered laughter. "Who's there?"

"It's I, friend . . ." answers an old man's voice.

"But who are you?"

"I . . . a traveller."

"What sort of traveller?" the watchman cries angrily, trying to disguise his terror by shouting. "What the devil do you want here? You go prowling about the graveyard at night, you ruffian!"

"You don't say it's a graveyard here?"

"Why, what else? Of course it's the graveyard! Don't you see it is?"

"O-o-oh . . . Queen of Heaven!" there is a sound of an old man sighing. "I see nothing, my good soul, nothing. Oh the darkness, the darkness! You can't see your hand before your face, it is dark, friend. O-o-oh. . ."

"But who are you?"

"I am a pilgrim, friend, a wandering man."

"The devils, the nightbirds. . . . Nice sort of pilgrims! They are drunkards . . ." mutters the watchman, reassured by the tone and sighs of the stranger. "One's tempted to sin by you. They drink the day away and prowl about at night. But I fancy I heard you were not alone; it sounded like two or three of you."

"I am alone, friend, alone. Quite alone. O-o-oh our sins. . . ."

The watchman stumbles up against the man and stops.

"How did you get here?" he asks.

"I have lost my way, good man. I was walking to the Mitrievsky Mill and I lost my way."

"Whew! Is this the road to Mitrievsky Mill? You sheepshead! For the Mitrievsky Mill you must keep much more to the left, straight out of the town along the high road. You have been drinking and have gone a couple of miles out of your way. You must have had a drop in the town."

"I did, friend . . . Truly I did; I won't hide my sins. But how am I to go now?"

"Go straight on and on along this avenue till you can go no farther, and then turn at once to the left and go till you have crossed the whole graveyard right to the gate. There will be a gate there. . . . Open it and go with God's blessing. Mind you don't fall into the ditch. And when you are out of the graveyard you go all the way by the fields till you come out on the main road."

"God give you health, friend. May the Queen of Heaven save you and have mercy on you. You might take me along, good man! Be merciful! Lead me to the gate."

"As though I had the time to waste! Go by yourself!"

"Be merciful! I'll pray for you. I can't see anything; one can't see one's hand before one's face, friend. . . . It's so dark, so dark! Show me the way, sir!"

"As though I had the time to take you about; if I were to play the nurse to everyone I should never have done."

"For Christ's sake, take me! I can't see, and I am afraid to go alone through the graveyard. It's terrifying, friend, it's terrifying; I am afraid, good man."

"There's no getting rid of you," sighs the watchman. "All right then, come along."

The watchman and the traveller go on together. They walk shoulder to shoulder in silence. A damp, cutting wind blows straight into their faces and the unseen trees murmuring and rustling scatter big drops upon them. . . . The path is almost entirely covered with puddles.

"There is one thing passes my understanding," says the watchman after a prolonged silence - "how you got here. The gate's locked. Did you climb over the wall? If you did climb over the wall, that's the last thing you would expect of an old man."

"I don't know, friend, I don't know. I can't say myself how I got here. It's a visitation. A chastisement of the Lord. Truly a visitation, the evil one confounded me. So you are a watchman here, friend?"

"Yes."

"The only one for the whole graveyard?"

There is such a violent gust of wind that both stop for a minute. Waiting till the violence of the wind abates, the watchman answers:

"There are three of us, but one is lying ill in a fever and the other's asleep. He and I take turns about."

"Ah, to be sure, friend. What a wind! The dead must hear it! It howls like a wild beast! O-o-oh."

"And where do you come from?"

"From a distance, friend. I am from Vologda, a long way off. I go from one holy place to another and pray for people. Save me and have mercy upon me, O Lord."

The watchman stops for a minute to light his pipe. He stoops down behind the traveller's back and lights several matches. The gleam of the first match lights up for one instant a bit of the avenue on the right, a white tombstone with an angel, and a dark cross; the light of the second match, flaring up brightly and extinguished by the wind, flashes like lightning on the left side, and from the darkness nothing stands out but the angle of some sort of trellis; the third match throws light to right and to left, revealing the white tombstone, the dark cross, and the trellis round a child's grave.

"The departed sleep; the dear ones sleep!" the stranger mutters, sighing loudly. "They all sleep alike, rich and poor, wise and foolish, good and wicked. They are of the same value now. And they will sleep till the last trump. The Kingdom of Heaven and peace eternal be theirs."

"Here we are walking along now, but the time will come when we shall be lying here ourselves," says the watchman.

"To be sure, to be sure, we shall all. There is no man who will not die. O-o-oh. Our doings are wicked, our thoughts are deceitful! Sins, sins! My soul accursed, ever covetous, my belly greedy and lustful! I have angered the Lord and there is no salvation for me in this world and the next. I am deep in sins like a worm in the earth."

"Yes, and you have to die."

"You are right there."

"Death is easier for a pilgrim than for fellows like us,"

says the watchman.

"There are pilgrims of different sorts. There are the real ones who are God-fearing men and watch over their own souls, and there are such as stray about the graveyard at night and are a delight to the devils. . . Ye-es! There's one who is a pilgrim could give you a crack on the pate with an axe if he liked and knock the breath out of you."

"What are you talking like that for?"

"Oh, nothing . . . Why, I fancy here's the gate. Yes, it is. Open it, good man."

The watchman, feeling his way, opens the gate, leads the pilgrim out by the sleeve, and says:

"Here's the end of the graveyard. Now you must keep on through the open fields till you get to the main road. Only close here there will be the boundary ditch - don't fall in. . . . And when you come out on to the road, turn to the right, and keep on till you reach the mill. . . ."

"O-o-oh!" sighs the pilgrim after a pause, "and now I am thinking that I have no cause to go to Mitrievsky Mill. . . . Why the devil should I go there? I had better stay a bit with you here, sir. . . ."

"What do you want to stay with me for?"

"Oh . . . it's merrier with you! . . . ."

"So you've found a merry companion, have you? You, pilgrim, are fond of a joke I see. . . ."

Anton Chekhov

"To be sure I am," says the stranger, with a hoarse chuckle. "Ah, my dear good man, I bet you will remember the pilgrim many a long year!"

"Why should I remember you?"

"Why I've got round you so smartly. . . . Am I a pilgrim? I am not a pilgrim at all."

"What are you then?"

"A dead man. . . . I've only just got out of my coffin. . . . Do you remember Gubaryev, the locksmith, who hanged himself in carnival week? Well, I am Gubaryev himself! . . ."

"Tell us something else!"

The watchman does not believe him, but he feels all over such a cold, oppressive terror that he starts off and begins hurriedly feeling for the gate.

"Stop, where are you off to?" says the stranger, clutching him by the arm. "Aie, aie, aie . . . what a fellow you are! How can you leave me all alone?"

"Let go!" cries the watchman, trying to pull his arm away.

"Sto-op! I bid you stop and you stop. Don't struggle, you dirty dog! If you want to stay among the living, stop and hold your tongue till I tell you. It's only that I don't care to spill blood or you would have been a dead man long ago, you scurvy rascal. . . . Stop!"

The watchman's knees give way under him. In his

terror he shuts his eyes, and trembling all over huddles close to the wall. He would like to call out, but he knows his cries would not reach any living thing. The stranger stands beside him and holds him by the arm. . .

Three minutes pass in silence.

"One's in a fever, another's asleep, and the third is seeing pilgrims on their way," mutters the stranger. "Capital watchmen, they are worth their salary! Ye-es, brother, thieves have always been cleverer than watchmen! Stand still, don't stir. . . ."

Five minutes, ten minutes pass in silence. All at once the wind brings the sound of a whistle.

"Well, now you can go," says the stranger, releasing the watchman's arm. "Go and thank God you are alive!"

The stranger gives a whistle too, runs away from the gate, and the watchman hears him leap over the ditch.

With a foreboding of something very dreadful in his heart, the watchman, still trembling with terror, opens the gate irresolutely and runs back with his eyes shut.

At the turning into the main avenue he hears hurried footsteps, and someone asks him, in a hissing voice: "Is that you, Timofey? Where is Mitka?"

And after running the whole length of the main avenue he notices a little dim light in the darkness. The nearer he gets to the light the more frightened he is and the stronger his foreboding of evil.

Anton Chekhov

"It looks as though the light were in the church," he thinks. "And how can it have come there? Save me and have mercy on me, Queen of Heaven! And that it is."

The watchman stands for a minute before the broken window and looks with horror towards the altar. . . . A little wax candle which the thieves had forgotten to put out flickers in the wind that bursts in at the window and throws dim red patches of light on the vestments flung about and a cupboard overturned on the floor, on numerous footprints near the high altar and the altar of offerings.

A little time passes and the howling wind sends floating over the churchyard the hurried uneven clangs of the alarm-bell. . . .

IN THE COURT

AT the district town of N. in the cinnamon-coloured government house in which the Zemstvo, the sessional meetings of the justices of the peace, the Rural Board, the Liquor Board, the Military Board, and many others sit by turns, the Circuit Court was in session on one of the dull days of autumn. Of the above-mentioned cinnamon-coloured house a local official had wittily observed:

"Here is Justitia, here is Policia, here is Militia - a regular boarding school of high-born young ladies."

But, as the saying is, "Too many cooks spoil the broth," and probably that is why the house strikes, oppresses, and overwhelms a fresh unofficial visitor with its dismal barrack-like appearance, its decrepit condition, and the complete absence of any kind of comfort, external or internal. Even on the brightest spring days it seems wrapped in a dense shade, and on clear moonlight nights, when the trees and the little dwelling-houses merged in one blur of shadow seem plunged in quiet slumber, it alone absurdly and inappropriately towers, an oppressive mass of stone, above the modest landscape, spoils the general harmony, and keeps sleepless vigil as though it could not escape from burdensome memories of past unforgiven sins. Inside it is like a barn and extremely

Anton Chekhov

unattractive. It is strange to see how readily these elegant lawyers, members of committees, and marshals of nobility, who in their own homes will make a scene over the slightest fume from the stove, or stain on the floor, resign themselves here to whirring ventilation wheels, the disgusting smell of fumigating candles, and the filthy, forever perspiring walls.

The sitting of the circuit court began between nine and ten. The programme of the day was promptly entered upon, with noticeable haste. The cases came on one after another and ended quickly, like a church service without a choir, so that no mind could form a complete picture of all this parti-coloured mass of faces, movements, words, misfortunes, true sayings and lies, all racing by like a river in flood. . . . By two o'clock a great deal had been done: two prisoners had been sentenced to service in convict battalions, one of the privileged class had been sentenced to deprivation of rights and imprisonment, one had been acquitted, one case had been adjourned.

At precisely two o'clock the presiding judge announced that the case "of the peasant Nikolay Harlamov, charged with the murder of his wife," would next be heard. The composition of the court remained the same as it had been for the preceding case, except that the place of the defending counsel was filled by a new personage, a beardless young graduate in a coat with bright buttons. The president gave the order - "Bring in the prisoner!"

But the prisoner, who had been got ready beforehand, was already walking to his bench. He was a tall, thick-set peasant of about fifty-five, completely bald, with an apathetic, hairy face and a big red beard. He was followed by a frail-looking little soldier with a gun.

Just as he was reaching the bench the escort had a trifling mishap. He stumbled and dropped the gun out of his hands, but caught it at once before it touched the ground, knocking his knee violently against the butt end as he did so. A faint laugh was audible in the audience. Either from the pain or perhaps from shame at his awkwardness the soldier flushed a dark red.

After the customary questions to the prisoner, the shuffling of the jury, the calling over and swearing in of the witnesses, the reading of the charge began. The narrow-chested, pale-faced secretary, far too thin for his uniform, and with sticking plaster on his check, read it in a low, thick bass, rapidly like a sacristan, without raising or dropping his voice, as though afraid of exerting his lungs; he was seconded by the ventilation wheel whirring indefatigably behind the judge's table, and the result was a sound that gave a drowsy, narcotic character to the stillness of the hall.

The president, a short-sighted man, not old but with an extremely exhausted face, sat in his armchair without stirring and held his open hand near his brow as though screening his eyes from the sun. To the droning of the ventilation wheel and the secretary he meditated. When the secretary paused for an instant to take breath on beginning a new page, he suddenly started and looked round at the court with lustreless eyes, then bent down to the ear of the judge next to him and asked with a sigh:

"Are you putting up at Demyanov's, Matvey Petrovitch?"

Anton Chekhov

"Yes, at Demyanov's," answered the other, starting too.

"Next time I shall probably put up there too. It's really impossible to put up at Tipyakov's! There's noise and uproar all night! Knocking, coughing, children crying. . . . It's impossible!"

The assistant prosecutor, a fat, well-nourished, dark man with gold spectacles, with a handsome, well-groomed beard, sat motionless as a statue, with his cheek propped on his fist, reading Byron's "Cain." His eyes were full of eager attention and his eyebrows rose higher and higher with wonder. . . . From time to time he dropped back in his chair, gazed without interest straight before him for a minute, and then buried himself in his reading again. The council for the defence moved the blunt end of his pencil about the table and mused with his head on one side. . . . His youthful face expressed nothing but the frigid, immovable boredom which is commonly seen on the face of schoolboys and men on duty who are forced from day to day to sit in the same place, to see the same faces, the same walls. He felt no excitement about the speech he was to make, and indeed what did that speech amount to? On instructions from his superiors in accordance with long-established routine he would fire it off before the jurymen, without passion or ardour, feeling that it was colourless and boring, and then - gallop through the mud and the rain to the station, thence to the town, shortly to receive instructions to go off again to some district to deliver another speech. . . . It was a bore!

At first the prisoner turned pale and coughed nervously into his sleeve, but soon the stillness, the general monotony and boredom infected him too. He looked with dull-witted respectfulness at the judges' uniforms, at the weary faces of the jurymen, and blinked calmly. The surroundings and procedure of the court, the expectation of which had so weighed on his soul while he was awaiting them in prison, now had the most soothing effect on him. What he met here was not at all what he could have expected. The charge of murder hung over him, and yet here he met with neither threatening faces nor indignant looks nor loud phrases about retribution nor sympathy for his extraordinary fate; not one of those who were judging him looked at him with interest or for long. . . . The dingy windows and walls, the voice of the secretary, the attitude of the prosecutor were all saturated with official indifference and produced an atmosphere of frigidity, as though the murderer were simply an official property, or as though he were not being judged by living men, but by some unseen machine, set going, goodness knows how or by whom. . . .

The peasant, reassured, did not understand that the men here were as accustomed to the dramas and tragedies of life and were as blunted by the sight of them as hospital attendants are at the sight of death, and that the whole horror and hopelessness of his position lay just in this mechanical indifference. It seemed that if he were not to sit quietly but to get up and begin beseeching, appealing with tears for their mercy, bitterly repenting, that if he were to die of despair - it would all be shattered against blunted nerves and the callousness of custom, like waves against a rock.

When the secretary finished, the president for some reason passed his hands over the table before him, looked for some time with his eyes screwed up towards

Anton Chekhov

the prisoner, and then asked, speaking languidly:

"Prisoner at the bar, do you plead guilty to having murdered your wife on the evening of the ninth of June?"

"No, sir," answered the prisoner, getting up and holding his gown over his chest.

After this the court proceeded hurriedly to the examination of witnesses. Two peasant women and five men and the village policeman who had made the enquiry were questioned. All of them, mud-bespattered, exhausted with their long walk and waiting in the witnesses' room, gloomy and dispirited, gave the same evidence. They testified that Harlamov lived "well" with his old woman, like anyone else; that he never beat her except when he had had a drop; that on the ninth of June when the sun was setting the old woman had been found in the porch with her skull broken; that beside her in a pool of blood lay an axe. When they looked for Nikolay to tell him of the calamity he was not in his hut or in the streets. They ran all over the village, looking for him. They went to all the pothouses and huts, but could not find him. He had disappeared, and two days later came of his own accord to the police office, pale, with his clothes torn, trembling all over. He was bound and put in the lock-up.

"Prisoner," said the president, addressing Harlamov, "cannot you explain to the court where you were during the three days following the murder?"

"I was wandering about the fields. . . . Neither eating nor drinking . . . ."

"Why did you hide yourself, if it was not you that committed the murder?

"I was frightened. . . . I was afraid I might be judged guilty. . . ."

"Aha! . . . Good, sit down!"

The last to be examined was the district doctor who had made a post-mortem on the old woman. He told the court all that he remembered of his report at the post-mortem and all that he had succeeded in thinking of on his way to the court that morning. The president screwed up his eyes at his new glossy black suit, at his foppish cravat, at his moving lips; he listened and in his mind the languid thought seemed to spring up of itself:

"Everyone wears a short jacket nowadays, why has he had his made long? Why long and not short?"

The circumspect creak of boots was audible behind the president's back. It was the assistant prosecutor going up to the table to take some papers.

"Mihail Vladimirovitch," said the assistant prosecutor, bending down to the president's ear, "amazingly slovenly the way that Koreisky conducted the investigation. The prisoner's brother was not examined, the village elder was not examined, there's no making anything out of his description of the hut. . . ."

"It can't be helped, it can't be helped," said the president, sinking back in his chair. "He's a wreck . . . dropping to bits!"

"By the way," whispered the assistant prosecutor, "look at the audience, in the front row, the third from the right . . . a face like an actor's . . . that's the local Croesus. He has a fortune of something like fifty thousand."

"Really? You wouldn't guess it from his appearance. . . . Well, dear boy, shouldn't we have a break?"

"We will finish the case for the prosecution, and then. . . ."

"As you think best. . . . Well?" the president raised his eyes to the doctor. "So you consider that death was instantaneous?"

"Yes, in consequence of the extent of the injury to the brain substance. . . ."

When the doctor had finished, the president gazed into the space between the prosecutor and the counsel for the defence and suggested:

"Have you any questions to ask?"

The assistant prosecutor shook his head negatively, without lifting his eyes from "Cain"; the counsel for the defence unexpectedly stirred and, clearing his throat, asked:

"Tell me, doctor, can you from the dimensions of the wound form any theory as to . . . as to the mental condition of the criminal? That is, I mean, does the extent of the injury justify the supposition that the accused was suffering from temporary aberration?"

The president raised his drowsy indifferent eyes to the counsel for the defence. The assistant prosecutor tore himself from "Cain," and looked at the president. They merely looked, but there was no smile, no surprise, no perplexity-their faces expressed nothing.

"Perhaps," the doctor hesitated, "if one considers the force with which . . . er - er - er . . . the criminal strikes the blow. . . . However, excuse me, I don't quite understand your question. . . ."

The counsel for the defence did not get an answer to his question, and indeed he did not feel the necessity of one. It was clear even to himself that that question had strayed into his mind and found utterance simply through the effect of the stillness, the boredom, the whirring ventilator wheels.

When they had got rid of the doctor the court rose to examine the "material evidences." The first thing examined was the full-skirted coat, upon the sleeve of which there was a dark brownish stain of blood. Harlamov on being questioned as to the origin of the stain stated:

"Three days before my old woman's death Penkov bled his horse. I was there; I was helping to be sure, and . . . and got smeared with it. . . ."

"But Penkov has just given evidence that he does not remember that you were present at the bleeding. . . ."

"I can't tell about that."

"Sit down."

They proceeded to examine the axe with which the old woman had been murdered.

"That's not my axe," the prisoner declared.

"Whose is it, then?"

"I can't tell . . . I hadn't an axe. . . ."

"A peasant can't get on for a day without an axe. And your neighbour Ivan Timofeyitch, with whom you mended a sledge, has given evidence that it is your axe. . . ."

"I can't say about that, but I swear before God (Harlamov held out his hand before him and spread out the fingers), before the living God. And I don't remember how long it is since I did have an axe of my own. I did have one like that only a bit smaller, but my son Prohor lost it. Two years before he went into the army, he drove off to fetch wood, got drinking with the fellows, and lost it. . . ."

"Good, sit down."

This systematic distrust and disinclination to hear him probably irritated and offended Harlamov. He blinked and red patches came out on his cheekbones.

"I swear in the sight of God," he went on, craning his neck forward. "If you don't believe me, be pleased to ask my son Prohor. Proshka, what did you do with the axe?" he suddenly asked in a rough voice, turning abruptly to the soldier escorting him. "Where is it?"

It was a painful moment! Everyone seemed to wince

and as it were shrink together. The same fearful, incredible thought flashed like lightning through every head in the court, the thought of possibly fatal coincidence, and not one person in the court dared to look at the soldier's face. Everyone refused to trust his thought and believed that he had heard wrong.

"Prisoner, conversation with the guards is forbidden . . ." the president made haste to say.

No one saw the escort's face, and horror passed over the hall unseen as in a mask. The usher of the court got up quietly from his place and tiptoeing with his hand held out to balance himself went out of the court. Half a minute later there came the muffled sounds and footsteps that accompany the change of guard.

All raised their heads and, trying to look as though nothing had happened, went on with their work. . . .

Anton Chekhov

BOOTS

A PIANO-TUNER called Murkin, a close-shaven man with a yellow face, with a nose stained with snuff, and cotton-wool in his ears, came out of his hotel-room into the passage, and in a cracked voice cried: "Semyon! Waiter!"

And looking at his frightened face one might have supposed that the ceiling had fallen in on him or that he had just seen a ghost in his room.

"Upon my word, Semyon!" he cried, seeing the attendant running towards him. "What is the meaning of it? I am a rheumatic, delicate man and you make me go barefoot! Why is it you don't give me my boots all this time? Where are they?"

Semyon went into Murkin's room, looked at the place where he was in the habit of putting the boots he had cleaned, and scratched his head: the boots were not there.

"Where can they be, the damned things?" Semyon brought out. "I fancy I cleaned them in the evening and put them here. . . . H'm! . . . Yesterday, I must own, I had a drop. . . . I must have put them in another room, I suppose. That must be it, Afanasy Yegoritch, they are in another room! There are lots of boots, and how the devil is one to know them apart when one is drunk and does not know what one is doing? . . . I must have taken them in to the lady that's next door . . . the actress. . . ."

"And now, if you please, I am to go in to a lady and disturb her all through you! Here, if you please, through this foolishness I am to wake up a respectable woman."

Sighing and coughing, Murkin went to the door of the next room andcautiously tapped.

"Who's there?" he heard a woman's voice a minute later.

"It's I!" Murkin began in a plaintive voice, standing in the attitude of a cavalier addressing a lady of the highest society. "Pardon my disturbing you, madam, but I am a man in delicate health, rheumatic . . . . The doctors, madam, have ordered me to keep my feet warm, especially as I have to go at once to tune the piano at Madame la Generale Shevelitsyn's. I can't go to her barefoot."

"But what do you want? What piano?"

"Not a piano, madam; it is in reference to boots! Semyon, stupid fellow, cleaned my boots and put them by mistake in your room. Be so extremely kind, madam, as to give me my boots!"

There was a sound of rustling, of jumping off the bed and the flapping of slippers, after which the door opened slightly and a plump feminine hand flung at Murkin's feet a pair of boots. The piano-tuner thanked

Anton Chekhov

her and went into his own room.

"Odd . . ." he muttered, putting on the boots, "it seems as though this is not the right boot. Why, here are two left boots! Both are for the left foot! I say, Semyon, these are not my boots! My boots have red tags and no patches on them, and these are in holes and have no tags."

Semyon picked up the boots, turned them over several times before his eyes, and frowned.

"Those are Pavel Alexandritch's boots," he grumbled, squinting at them. He squinted with the left eye.

"What Pavel Alexandritch?"

"The actor; he comes here every Tuesday. . . . He must have put on yours instead of his own. . . . So I must have put both pairs in her room, his and yours. Here's a go!"

"Then go and change them!"

"That's all right!" sniggered Semyon, "go and change them. . . . Where am I to find him now? He went off an hour ago. . . . Go and look for the wind in the fields!"

"Where does he live then?"

"Who can tell? He comes here every Tuesday, and where he lives I don't know. He comes and stays the night, and then you may wait till next Tuesday. . . ."

"There, do you see, you brute, what you have done? Why, what am I to do now? It is time I was at Madame la Generale Shevelitsyn's, you anathema! My feet are frozen!"

"You can change the boots before long. Put on these boots, go about in them till the evening, and in the evening go to the theatre. . . . Ask there for Blistanov, the actor. . . . If you don't care to go to the theatre, you will have to wait till next Tuesday; he only comes here on Tuesdays. . . ."

"But why are there two boots for the left foot?" asked the piano-tuner, picking up the boots with an air of disgust.

"What God has sent him, that he wears. Through poverty . . . where is an actor to get boots? I said to him 'What boots, Pavel Alexandritch! They are a positive disgrace!' and he said: 'Hold your peace,' says he, 'and turn pale! In those very boots,' says he, 'I have played counts and princes.' A queer lot! Artists, that's the only word for them! If I were the governor or anyone in command, I would get all these actors together and clap them all in prison."

Continually sighing and groaning and knitting his brows, Murkin drew the two left boots on to his feet, and set off, limping, to Madame la Generale Shevelitsyn's. He went about the town all day long tuning pianos, and all day long it seemed to him that everyone was looking at his feet and seeing his patched boots with heels worn down at the sides! Apart from his moral agonies he had to suffer physically also; the boots gave him a corn.

In the evening he was at the theatre. There was a performance of *Bluebeard*. It was only just before the last act, and then only thanks to the good offices of a man he knew who played a flute in the orchestra, that he gained admittance behind the scenes. Going to the men's dressing-room, he found there all the male performers. Some were changing their clothes, others were painting their faces, others were smoking. Bluebeard was standing with King Bobesh, showing him a revolver.

"You had better buy it," said Bluebeard. "I bought it at Kursk, a bargain, for eight roubles, but, there! I will let you have it for six. . . . A wonderfully good one!"

"Steady. . . . It's loaded, you know!"

"Can I see Mr. Blistanov?" the piano-tuner asked as he went in.

"I am he!" said Bluebeard, turning to him. "What do you want?"

"Excuse my troubling you, sir," began the piano-tuner in an imploring voice, "but, believe me, I am a man in delicate health, rheumatic. The doctors have ordered me to keep my feet warm . . ."

"But, speaking plainly, what do you want?"

"You see," said the piano-tuner, addressing Bluebeard. "Er . . . you stayed last night at Buhteyev's furnished apartments . . . No. 64 . . ."

"What's this nonsense?" said King Bobesh with a grin. "My wife is at No. 64."

"Your wife, sir? Delighted. . . ." Murkin smiled. "It

was she, your good lady, who gave me this gentleman's boots. . . . After this gentleman - " the piano-tuner indicated Blistanov - "had gone away I missed my boots. . . . I called the waiter, you know, and he said: 'I left your boots in the next room!' By mistake, being in a state of intoxication, he left my boots as well as yours at 64," said Murkin, turning to Blistanov, "and when you left this gentleman's lady you put on mine."

"What are you talking about?" said Blistanov, and he scowled. "Have you come here to libel me?"

"Not at all, sir - God forbid! You misunderstand me. What am I talking about? About boots! You did stay the night at No. 64, didn't you?"

"When?"

"Last night!"

"Why, did you see me there?"

"No, sir, I didn't see you," said Murkin in great confusion, sitting down and taking off the boots. "I did not see you, but this gentleman's lady threw out your boots here to me . . . instead of mine."

"What right have you, sir, to make such assertions? I say nothing about myself, but you are slandering a woman, and in the presence of her husband, too!"

A fearful hubbub arose behind the scenes. King Bobesh, the injured husband, suddenly turned crimson and brought his fist down upon the table with such violence that two actresses in the next dressing-room felt faint.

"And you believe it?" cried Bluebeard. "You believe this worthless rascal? O-oh! Would you like me to kill him like a dog? Would you like it? I will turn him into a beefsteak! I'll blow his brains out!"

And all the persons who were promenading that evening in the town park by the Summer theatre describe to this day how just before the fourth act they saw a man with bare feet, a yellow face, and terror-stricken eyes dart out of the theatre and dash along the principal avenue. He was pursued by a man in the costume of Bluebeard, armed with a revolver. What happened later no one saw. All that is known is that Murkin was confined to his bed for a fortnight after his acquaintance with Blistanov, and that to the words "I am a man in delicate health, rheumatic" he took to adding, "I am a wounded man. . . ."

JOY

IT was twelve o'clock at night.

Mitya Kuldarov, with excited face and ruffled hair, flew into his parents' flat, and hurriedly ran through all the rooms. His parents had already gone to bed. His sister was in bed, finishing the last page of a novel. His schoolboy brothers were asleep.

"Where have you come from?" cried his parents in amazement. "What is the matter with you?

"Oh, don't ask! I never expected it; no, I never expected it! It's . . . it's positively incredible!"

Mitya laughed and sank into an armchair, so overcome by happiness that he could not stand on his legs.

"It's incredible! You can't imagine! Look!"

His sister jumped out of bed and, throwing a quilt round her, went in to her brother. The schoolboys woke up.

"What's the matter? You don't look like yourself!"

"It's because I am so delighted, Mamma! Do you know, now all Russia knows of me! All Russia! Till

Anton Chekhov

now only you knew that there was a registration clerk called Dmitry Kuldarov, and now all Russia knows it! Mamma! Oh, Lord!"

Mitya jumped up, ran up and down all the rooms, and then sat down again.

"Why, what has happened? Tell us sensibly!"

"You live like wild beasts, you don't read the newspapers and take no notice of what's published, and there's so much that is interesting in the papers. If anything happens it's all known at once, nothing is hidden! How happy I am! Oh, Lord! You know it's only celebrated people whose names are published in the papers, and now they have gone and published mine!"

"What do you mean? Where?"

The papa turned pale. The mamma glanced at the holy image and crossed herself. The schoolboys jumped out of bed and, just as they were, in short nightshirts, went up to their brother.

"Yes! My name has been published! Now all Russia knows of me! Keep the paper, mamma, in memory of it! We will read it sometimes! Look!"

Mitya pulled out of his pocket a copy of the paper, gave it to his father, and pointed with his finger to a passage marked with blue pencil.

"Read it!"

The father put on his spectacles.

"Do read it!"

The mamma glanced at the holy image and crossed herself. The papa cleared his throat and began to read: "At eleven o'clock on the evening of the 29th of December, a registration clerk of the name of Dmitry Kuldarov . . ."

"You see, you see! Go on!"

". . . a registration clerk of the name of Dmitry Kuldarov, coming from the beershop in Kozihin's buildings in Little Bronnaia in an intoxicated condition. . ."

"That's me and Semyon Petrovitch. . . . It's all described exactly! Go on! Listen!"

". . . intoxicated condition, slipped and fell under a horse belonging to a sledge-driver, a peasant of the village of Durikino in the Yuhnovsky district, called Ivan Drotov. The frightened horse, stepping over Kuldarov and drawing the sledge over him, together with a Moscow merchant of the second guild called Stepan Lukov, who was in it, dashed along the street and was caught by some house-porters. Kuldarov, at first in an unconscious condition, was taken to the police station and there examined by the doctor. The blow he had received on the back of his head. . ."

"It was from the shaft, papa. Go on! Read the rest!"

". . . he had received on the back of his head turned out not to be serious. The incident was duly reported. Medical aid was given to the injured man. . . ."

"They told me to foment the back of my head with cold water. You have read it now? Ah! So you see. Now it's all over Russia! Give it here!"

Mitya seized the paper, folded it up and put it into his pocket.

"I'll run round to the Makarovs and show it to them. . . . I must show it to the Ivanitskys too, Natasya Ivanovna, and Anisim Vassilyitch. . . . I'll run! Good-bye!"

Mitya put on his cap with its cockade and, joyful and triumphant, ran into the street.

LADIES

FYODOR PETROVITCH the Director of Elementary Schools in the N. District, who considered himself a just and generous man, was one day interviewing in his office a schoolmaster called Vremensky.

"No, Mr. Vremensky," he was saying, "your retirement is inevitable. You cannot continue your work as a schoolmaster with a voice like that! How did you come to lose it?"

"I drank cold beer when I was in a perspiration. . ." hissed the schoolmaster.

"What a pity! After a man has served fourteen years, such a calamity all at once! The idea of a career being ruined by such a trivial thing. What are you intending to do now?"

The schoolmaster made no answer.

"Are you a family man?" asked the director.

"A wife and two children, your Excellency . . ." hissed the schoolmaster.

A silence followed. The director got up from the table and walked to and fro in perturbation.

Anton Chekhov

"I cannot think what I am going to do with you!" he said. "A teacher you cannot be, and you are not yet entitled to a pension. . . . To abandon you to your fate, and leave you to do the best you can, is rather awkward. We look on you as one of our men, you have served fourteen years, so it is our business to help you. . . . But how are we to help you? What can I do for you? Put yourself in my place: what can I do for you?"

A silence followed; the director walked up and down, still thinking, and Vremensky, overwhelmed by his trouble, sat on the edge of his chair, and he, too, thought. All at once the director began beaming, and even snapped his fingers.

"I wonder I did not think of it before!" he began rapidly. "Listen, this is what I can offer you. Next week our secretary at the Home is retiring. If you like, you can have his place! There you are!"

Vremensky, not expecting such good fortune, beamed too.

"That's capital," said the director. "Write the application to-day."

Dismissing Vremensky, Fyodor Petrovitch felt relieved and even gratified: the bent figure of the hissing schoolmaster was no longer confronting him, and it was agreeable to recognize that in offering a vacant post to Vremensky he had acted fairly and conscientiously, like a good-hearted and thoroughly decent person. But this agreeable state of mind did not last long. When he went home and sat down to dinner his wife, Nastasya Ivanovna, said suddenly:

"Oh yes, I was almost forgetting! Nina Sergeyevna came to see me yesterday and begged for your interest on behalf of a young man. I am told there is a vacancy in our Home. . . ."

"Yes, but the post has already been promised to someone else," said the director, and he frowned. "And you know my rule: I never give posts through patronage."

"I know, but for Nina Sergeyevna, I imagine, you might make an exception. She loves us as though we were relations, and we have never done anything for her. And don't think of refusing, Fedya! You will wound both her and me with your whims."

"Who is it that she is recommending?"

"Polzuhin!"

"What Polzuhin? Is it that fellow who played Tchatsky at the party on New Year's Day? Is it that gentleman? Not on any account!"

The director left off eating.

"Not on any account!" he repeated. "Heaven preserve us!"

"But why not?"

"Understand, my dear, that if a young man does not set to work directly, but through women, he must be good for nothing! Why doesn't he come to me himself?"

After dinner the director lay on the sofa in his study

and began reading the letters and newspapers he had received.

"Dear Fyodor Petrovitch," wrote the wife of the Mayor of the town. "You once said that I knew the human heart and understood people. Now you have an opportunity of verifying this in practice. K. N. Polzuhin, whom I know to be an excellent young man, will call upon you in a day or two to ask you for the post of secretary at our Home. He is a very nice youth. If you take an interest in him you will be convinced of it." And so on.

"On no account!" was the director's comment. "Heaven preserve me!"

After that, not a day passed without the director's receiving letters recommending Polzuhin. One fine morning Polzuhin himself, a stout young man with a close-shaven face like a jockey's, in a new black suit, made his appearance. . . .

"I see people on business not here but at the office," said the director drily, on hearing his request.

"Forgive me, your Excellency, but our common acquaintances advised me to come here."

"H'm!" growled the director, looking with hatred at the pointed toes of the young man's shoes. "To the best of my belief your father is a man of property and you are not in want," he said. "What induces you to ask for this post? The salary is very trifling!"

"It's not for the sake of the salary. . . . It's a government post, any way . . ."

"H'm. . . . It strikes me that within a month you will be sick of the job and you will give it up, and meanwhile there are candidates for whom it would be a career for life. There are poor men for whom . . ."

"I shan't get sick of it, your Excellency," Polzuhin interposed. "Honour bright, I will do my best!"

It was too much for the director.

"Tell me," he said, smiling contemptuously, "why was it you didn't apply to me direct but thought fitting instead to trouble ladies as a preliminary?"

"I didn't know that it would be disagreeable to you," Polzuhin answered, and he was embarrassed. "But, your Excellency, if you attach no significance to letters of recommendation, I can give you a testimonial. . . ."

He drew from his pocket a letter and handed it to the director. At the bottom of the testimonial, which was written in official language and handwriting, stood the signature of the Governor. Everything pointed to the Governor's having signed it unread, simply to get rid of some importunate lady.

"There's nothing for it, I bow to his authority. . . I obey . . ." said the director, reading the testimonial, and he heaved a sigh.

"Send in your application to-morrow. . . . There's nothing to be done. . . ."

And when Polzuhin had gone out, the director abandoned himself to a feeling of repulsion.

"Sneak!" he hissed, pacing from one corner to the other. "He has got what he wanted, one way or the other, the good-for-nothing toady! Making up to the ladies! Reptile! Creature!"

The director spat loudly in the direction of the door by which Polzuhin had departed, and was immediately overcome with embarrassment, for at that moment a lady, the wife of the Superintendent of the Provincial Treasury, walked in at the door.

"I've come for a tiny minute . . . a tiny minute. . ." began the lady. "Sit down, friend, and listen to me attentively. . . . Well, I've been told you have a post vacant. . . . To-day or to-morrow you will receive a visit from a young man called Polzuhin. . . ."

The lady chattered on, while the director gazed at her with lustreless, stupefied eyes like a man on the point of fainting, gazed and smiled from politeness.

And the next day when Vremensky came to his office it was a long time before the director could bring himself to tell the truth. He hesitated, was incoherent, and could not think how to begin or what to say. He wanted to apologize to the schoolmaster, to tell him the whole truth, but his tongue halted like a drunkard's, his ears burned, and he was suddenly overwhelmed with vexation and resentment that he should have to play such an absurd part - in his own office, before his subordinate. He suddenly brought his fist down on the table, leaped up, and shouted angrily:

"I have no post for you! I have not, and that's all about it! Leave me in peace! Don't worry me! Be so good as to leave me alone!"

And he walked out of the office.

Anton Chekhov

A PECULIAR MAN

BETWEEN twelve and one at night a tall gentleman, wearing a top-hat and a coat with a hood, stops before the door of Marya Petrovna Koshkin, a midwife and an old maid. Neither face nor hand can be distinguished in the autumn darkness, but in the very manner of his coughing and the ringing of the bell a certain solidity, positiveness, and even impressiveness can be discerned. After the third ring the door opens and Marya Petrovna herself appears. She has a man's overcoat flung on over her white petticoat. The little lamp with the green shade which she holds in her hand throws a greenish light over her sleepy, freckled face, her scraggy neck, and the lank, reddish hair that strays from under her cap.

"Can I see the midwife?" asks the gentleman.

"I am the midwife. What do you want?"

The gentleman walks into the entry and Marya Petrovna sees facing her a tall, well-made man, no longer young, but with a handsome, severe face and bushy whiskers.

"I am a collegiate assessor, my name is Kiryakov," he says. "I came to fetch you to my wife. Only please make haste."

"Very good . . ." the midwife assents. "I'll dress at once, and I must trouble you to wait for me in the parlour."

Kiryakov takes off his overcoat and goes into the parlour. The greenish light of the lamp lies sparsely on the cheap furniture in patched white covers, on the pitiful flowers and the posts on which ivy is trained . . . . There is a smell of geranium and carbolic. The little clock on the wall ticks timidly, as though abashed at the presence of a strange man.

"I am ready," says Marya Petrovna, coming into the room five minutes later, dressed, washed, and ready for action. "Let us go."

"Yes, you must make haste," says Kiryakov. "And, by the way, it is not out of place to enquire - what do you ask for your services?"

"I really don't know . . ." says Marya Petrovna with an embarrassed smile. "As much as you will give."

"No, I don't like that," says Kiryakov, looking coldly and steadily at the midwife. "An arrangement beforehand is best. I don't want to take advantage of you and you don't want to take advantage of me. To avoid misunderstandings it is more sensible for us to make an arrangement beforehand."

"I really don't know - there is no fixed price."

"I work myself and am accustomed to respect the work of others. I don't like injustice. It will be equally unpleasant to me if I pay you too little, or if you demand from me too much, and so I insist on your naming your charge."

"Well, there are such different charges."

"H'm. In view of your hesitation, which I fail to understand, I am constrained to fix the sum myself. I can give you two roubles."

"Good gracious! . . . Upon my word! . . ." says Marya Petrovna, turning crimson and stepping back. "I am really ashamed. Rather than take two roubles I will come for nothing . . . . Five roubles, if you like."

"Two roubles, not a kopeck more. I don't want to take advantage of you, but I do not intend to be overcharged."

"As you please, but I am not coming for two roubles. . . ."

"But by law you have not the right to refuse."

"Very well, I will come for nothing."

"I won't have you for nothing. All work ought to receive remuneration. I work myself and I understand that. . . ."

"I won't come for two roubles," Marya Petrovna answers mildly. "I'll come for nothing if you like."

"In that case I regret that I have troubled you for nothing. . . . I have the honour to wish you good-bye."

"Well, you are a man!" says Marya Petrovna, seeing him into the entry. "I will come for three roubles if that will satisfy you."

Kiryakov frowns and ponders for two full minutes, looking with concentration on the floor, then he says resolutely, "No," and goes out into the street. The astonished and disconcerted midwife fastens the door after him and goes back into her bedroom.

"He's good-looking, respectable, but how queer, God bless the man! . . ." she thinks as she gets into bed.

But in less than half an hour she hears another ring; she gets up and sees the same Kiryakov again.

"Extraordinary the way things are mismanaged. Neither the chemist, nor the police, nor the house-porters can give me the address of a midwife, and so I am under the necessity of assenting to your terms. I will give you three roubles, but . . . I warn you beforehand that when I engage servants or receive any kind of services, I make an arrangement beforehand in order that when I pay there may be no talk of extras, tips, or anything of the sort. Everyone ought to receive what is his due."

Marya Petrovna has not listened to Kiryakov for long, but already she feels that she is bored and repelled by him, that his even, measured speech lies like a weight on her soul. She dresses and goes out into the street with him. The air is still but cold, and the sky is so overcast that the light of the street lamps is hardly visible. The sloshy snow squelches under their feet. The midwife looks intently but does not see a cab.

"I suppose it is not far?" she asks.

"No, not far," Kiryakov answers grimly.

They walk down one turning, a second, a third. . . .
Kiryakov strides along, and even in his step his
respectability and positiveness is apparent.

"What awful weather!" the midwife observes to him.

But he preserves a dignified silence, and it is noticeable that he tries to step on the smooth stones to avoid
spoiling his goloshes. At last after a long walk the midwife steps into the entry; from which she can see a big
decently furnished drawing-room. There is not a soul
in the rooms, even in the bedroom where the woman is
lying in labour. . . . The old women and relations who
flock in crowds to every confinement are not to be
seen. The cook rushes about alone, with a scared and
vacant face. There is a sound of loud groans.

Three hours pass. Marya Petrovna sits by the mother's
bedside and whispers to her. The two women have
already had time to make friends, they have got to
know each other, they gossip, they sigh together. . . .

"You mustn't talk," says the midwife anxiously, and at
the same time she showers questions on her.

Then the door opens and Kiryakov himself comes
quietly and stolidly into the room. He sits down in the
chair and strokes his whiskers. Silence reigns. Marya
Petrovna looks timidly at his handsome, passionless,
wooden face and waits for him to begin to talk, but he
remains absolutely silent and absorbed in thought.
After waiting in vain, the midwife makes up her mind
to begin herself, and utters a phrase commonly used at
confinements.

"Well now, thank God, there is one human being more in the world!"

"Yes, that's agreeable," said Kiryakov, preserving the wooden expression of his face, "though indeed, on the other hand, to have more children you must have more money. The baby is not born fed and clothed."

A guilty expression comes into the mother's face, as though she had brought a creature into the world without permission or through idle caprice. Kiryakov gets up with a sigh and walks with solid dignity out of the room.

"What a man, bless him!" says the midwife to the mother. "He's so stern and does not smile."

The mother tells her that *he* is always like that. . . . He is honest, fair, prudent, sensibly economical, but all that to such an exceptional degree that simple mortals feel suffocated by it. His relations have parted from him, the servants will not stay more than a month; they have no friends; his wife and children are always on tenterhooks from terror over every step they take. He does not shout at them nor beat them, his virtues are far more numerous than his defects, but when he goes out of the house they all feel better, and more at ease. Why it is so the woman herself cannot say.

"The basins must be properly washed and put away in the store cupboard," says Kiryakov, coming into the bedroom. "These bottles must be put away too: they may come in handy."

What he says is very simple and ordinary, but the midwife for some reason feels flustered. She begins to

Anton Chekhov

be afraid of the man and shudders every time she hears his footsteps. In the morning as she is preparing to depart she sees Kiryakov's little son, a pale, close-cropped schoolboy, in the dining-room drinking his tea. . . . Kiryakov is standing opposite him, saying in his flat, even voice:

"You know how to eat, you must know how to work too. You have just swallowed a mouthful but have not probably reflected that that mouthful costs money and money is obtained by work. You must eat and reflect. . . ."

The midwife looks at the boy's dull face, and it seems to her as though the very air is heavy, that a little more and the very walls will fall, unable to endure the crushing presence of the peculiar man. Beside herself with terror, and by now feeling a violent hatred for the man, Marya Petrovna gathers up her bundles and hurriedly departs.

Half-way home she remembers that she has forgotten to ask for her three roubles, but after stopping and thinking for a minute, with a wave of her hand, she goes on.

AT THE BARBER'S

MORNING. It is not yet seven o'clock, but Makar Kuzmitch Blyostken's shop is already open. The barber himself, an unwashed, greasy, but foppishly dressed youth of three and twenty, is busy clearing up; there is really nothing to be cleared away, but he is perspiring with his exertions. In one place he polishes with a rag, in another he scrapes with his finger or catches a bug and brushes it off the wall.

The barber's shop is small, narrow, and unclean. The log walls are hung with paper suggestive of a cabman's faded shirt. Between the two dingy, perspiring windows there is a thin, creaking, rickety door, above it, green from the damp, a bell which trembles and gives a sickly ring of itself without provocation. Glance into the looking-glass which hangs on one of the walls, and it distorts your countenance in all directions in the most merciless way! The shaving and haircutting is done before this looking-glass. On the little table, as greasy and unwashed as Makar Kuzmitch himself, there is everything: combs, scissors, razors, a ha'porth of wax for the moustache, a ha'porth of powder, a ha'porth of much watered eau de Cologne, and indeed the whole barber's shop is not worth more than fifteen kopecks.

There is a squeaking sound from the invalid bell and

an elderly man in a tanned sheepskin and high felt over-boots walks into the shop. His head and neck are wrapped in a woman's shawl.

This is Erast Ivanitch Yagodov, Makar Kuzmitch's godfather. At one time he served as a watchman in the Consistory, now he lives near the Red Pond and works as a locksmith.

"Makarushka, good-day, dear boy!" he says to Makar Kuzmitch, who is absorbed in tidying up.

They kiss each other. Yagodov drags his shawl off his head, crosses himself, and sits down.

"What a long way it is!" he says, sighing and clearing his throat. "It's no joke! From the Red Pond to the Kaluga gate."

"How are you?"

"In a poor way, my boy. I've had a fever."

"You don't say so! Fever!"

"Yes, I have been in bed a month; I thought I should die. I had extreme unction. Now my hair's coming out. The doctor says I must be shaved. He says the hair will grow again strong. And so, I thought, I'll go to Makar. Better to a relation than to anyone else. He will do it better and he won't take anything for it. It's rather far, that's true, but what of it? It's a walk."

"I'll do it with pleasure. Please sit down."

With a scrape of his foot Makar Kuzmitch indicates a

chair. Yagodov sits down and looks at himself in the glass and is apparently pleased with his reflection: the looking-glass displays a face awry, with Kalmuck lips, a broad, blunt nose, and eyes in the forehead. Makar Kuzmitch puts round his client's shoulders a white sheet with yellow spots on it, and begins snipping with the scissors.

"I'll shave you clean to the skin!" he says.

"To be sure. So that I may look like a Tartar, like a bomb. The hair will grow all the thicker."

"How's auntie?"

"Pretty middling. The other day she went as midwife to the major's lady. They gave her a rouble."

"Oh, indeed, a rouble. Hold your ear."

"I am holding it. . . . Mind you don't cut me. Oy, you hurt! You are pulling my hair."

"That doesn't matter. We can't help that in our work. And how is Anna Erastovna?"

"My daughter? She is all right, she's skipping about. Last week on the Wednesday we betrothed her to Sheikin. Why didn't you come?"

The scissors cease snipping. Makar Kuzmitch drops his hands and asks in a fright:

"Who is betrothed?"

"Anna."

"How's that? To whom?"

"To Sheikin. Prokofy Petrovitch. His aunt's a housekeeper in Zlatoustensky Lane. She is a nice woman. Naturally we are all delighted, thank God. The wedding will be in a week. Mind you come; we will have a good time."

"But how's this, Erast Ivanitch?" says Makar Kuzmitch, pale, astonished, and shrugging his shoulders. "It's . . . it's utterly impossible. Why, Anna Erastovna . . . why I . . . why, I cherished sentiments for her, I had intentions. How could it happen?"

"Why, we just went and betrothed her. He's a good fellow."

Cold drops of perspiration come on the face of Makar Kuzmitch. He puts the scissors down on the table and begins rubbing his nose with his fist.

"I had intentions," he says. "It's impossible, Erast Ivanitch. I . . . I am in love with her and have made her the offer of my heart . . . . And auntie promised. I have always respected you as though you were my father. . . . I always cut your hair for nothing. . . . I have always obliged you, and when my papa died you took the sofa and ten roubles in cash and have never given them back. Do you remember?"

"Remember! of course I do. Only, what sort of a match would you be, Makar? You are nothing of a match. You've neither money nor position, your trade's a paltry one."

"And is Sheikin rich?"

"Sheikin is a member of a union. He has a thousand and a half lent on mortgage. So my boy . . . . It's no good talking about it, the thing's done. There is no altering it, Makarushka. You must look out for another bride. . . . The world is not so small. Come, cut away. Why are you stopping?"

Makar Kuzmitch is silent and remains motionless, then he takes a handkerchief out of his pocket and begins to cry.

"Come, what is it?" Erast Ivanitch comforts him. "Give over. Fie, he is blubbering like a woman! You finish my head and then cry. Take up the scissors!"

Makar Kuzmitch takes up the scissors, stares vacantly at them for a minute, then drops them again on the table. His hands are shaking.

"I can't," he says. "I can't do it just now. I haven't the strength! I am a miserable man! And she is miserable! We loved each other, we had given each other our promise and we have been separated by unkind people without any pity. Go away, Erast Ivanitch! I can't bear the sight of you."

"So I'll come to-morrow, Makarushka. You will finish me to-morrow."

"Right."

"You calm yourself and I will come to you early in the morning."

Erast Ivanitch has half his head shaven to the skin and looks like a convict. It is awkward to be left with a head like that, but there is no help for it. He wraps his head in the shawl and walks out of the barber's shop. Left alone, Makar Kuzmitch sits down and goes on quietly weeping.

Early next morning Erast Ivanitch comes again.

"What do you want?" Makar Kuzmitch asks him coldly.

"Finish cutting my hair, Makarushka. There is half the head left to do."

"Kindly give me the money in advance. I won't cut it for nothing."

Without saying a word Erast Ivanitch goes out, and to this day his hair is long on one side of the head and short on the other. He regards it as extravagance to pay for having his hair cut and is waiting for the hair to grow of itself on the shaven side.

He danced at the wedding in that condition.

AN INADVERTENCE

PYOTR PETROVITCH STRIZHIN, the nephew of Madame Ivanov, the colonel's widow - the man whose new goloshes were stolen last year, - came home from a christening party at two o'clock in the morning. To avoid waking the household he took off his things in the lobby, made his way on tiptoe to his room, holding his breath, and began getting ready for bed without lighting a candle.

Strizhin leads a sober and regular life. He has a sanctimonious expression of face, he reads nothing but religious and edifying books, but at the christening party, in his delight that Lyubov Spiridonovna had passed through her confinement successfully, he had permitted himself to drink four glasses of vodka and a glass of wine, the taste of which suggested something midway between vinegar and castor oil. Spirituous liquors are like sea-water and glory: the more you imbibe of them the greater your thirst. And now as he undressed, Strizhin was aware of an overwhelming craving for drink.

"I believe Dashenka has some vodka in the cupboard in the right-hand corner," he thought. "If I drink one wine-glassful, she won't notice it."

After some hesitation, overcoming his fears, Strizhin

went to the cupboard. Cautiously opening the door he felt in the right-hand corner for a bottle and poured out a wine-glassful, put the bottle back in its place, then, making the sign of the cross, drank it off. And immediately something like a miracle took place. Strizhin was flung back from the cupboard to the chest with fearful force like a bomb. There were flashes before his eyes, he felt as though he could not breathe, and all over his body he had a sensation as though he had fallen into a marsh full of leeches. It seemed to him as though, instead of vodka, he had swallowed dynamite, which blew up his body, the house, and the whole street. . . . His head, his arms, his legs - all seemed to be torn off and to be flying away somewhere to the devil, into space.

For some three minutes he lay on the chest, not moving and scarcely breathing, then he got up and asked himself:

"Where am I?"

The first thing of which he was clearly conscious on coming to himself was the pronounced smell of paraffin.

"Holy saints," he thought in horror, "it's paraffin I have drunk instead of vodka."

The thought that he had poisoned himself threw him into a cold shiver, then into a fever. That it was really poison that he had taken was proved not only by the smell in the room but also by the burning taste in his mouth, the flashes before his eyes, the ringing in his head, and the colicky pain in his stomach. Feeling the approach of death and not buoying himself up with false hopes, he wanted to say good-bye to those nearest to him, and made his way to Dashenka's bedroom (being a widower he had his sister-in-law called Dashenka, an old maid, living in the flat to keep house for him).

"Dashenka," he said in a tearful voice as he went into the bedroom, "dear Dashenka!"

Something grumbled in the darkness and uttered a deep sigh.

"Dashenka."

"Eh? What?" A woman's voice articulated rapidly. "Is that you, Pyotr Petrovitch? Are you back already? Well, what is it? What has the baby been christened? Who was godmother?"

"The godmother was Natalya Andreyevna Velikosvyetsky, and the godfather Pavel Ivanitch Bezsonnitsin. . . . I . . . I believe, Dashenka, I am dying. And the baby has been christened Olimpiada, in honour of their kind patroness. . . . I . . . I have just drunk paraffin, Dashenka!"

"What next! You don't say they gave you paraffin there?"

"I must own I wanted to get a drink of vodka without asking you, and . . . and the Lord chastised me: by accident in the dark I took paraffin. . . . What am I to do?"

Dashenka, hearing that the cupboard had been opened without her permission, grew more wide-awake. . . .

She quickly lighted a candle, jumped out of bed, and in her nightgown, a freckled, bony figure in curl-papers, padded with bare feet to the cupboard.

"Who told you you might?" she asked sternly, as she scrutinized the inside of the cupboard. "Was the vodka put there for you?"

"I . . . I haven't drunk vodka but paraffin, Dashenka . . ." muttered Strizhin, mopping the cold sweat on his brow.

"And what did you want to touch the paraffin for? That's nothing to do with you, is it? Is it put there for you? Or do you suppose paraffin costs nothing? Eh? Do you know what paraffin is now? Do you know?"

"Dear Dashenka," moaned Strizhin, "it's a question of life and death, and you talk about money!"

"He's drunk himself tipsy and now he pokes his nose into the cupboard!" cried Dashenka, angrily slamming the cupboard door. "Oh, the monsters, the tormentors! I'm a martyr, a miserable woman, no peace day or night! Vipers, basilisks, accursed Herods, may you suffer the same in the world to come! I am going to-morrow! I am a maiden lady and I won't allow you to stand before me in your underclothes! How dare you look at me when I am not dressed!"

And she went on and on. . . . Knowing that when Dashenka was enraged there was no moving her with prayers or vows or even by firing a cannon, Strizhin waved his hand in despair, dressed, and made up his mind to go to the doctor. But a doctor is only readily found when he is not wanted. After running through three streets and ringing five times at Dr. Tchepharyants's, and seven times at Dr. Bultyhin's, Strizhin raced off to a chemist's shop, thinking possibly the chemist could help him. There, after a long interval, a little dark and curly-headed chemist came out to him in his dressing gown, with drowsy eyes, and such a wise and serious face that it was positively terrifying.

"What do you want?" he asked in a tone in which only very wise and dignified chemists of Jewish persuasion can speak.

"For God's sake . . . I entreat you . . ." said Strizhin breathlessly, "give me something. I have just accidentally drunk paraffin, I am dying!"

"I beg you not to excite yourself and to answer the questions I am about to put to you. The very fact that you are excited prevents me from understanding you. You have drunk paraffin. Yes?"

"Yes, paraffin! Please save me!"

The chemist went coolly and gravely to the desk, opened a book, became absorbed in reading it. After reading a couple of pages he shrugged one shoulder and then the other, made a contemptuous grimace and, after thinking for a minute, went into the adjoining room. The clock struck four, and when it pointed to ten minutes past the chemist came back with another book and again plunged into reading.

"H'm," he said as though puzzled, "the very fact that you feel unwell shows you ought to apply to a doctor, not a chemist."

Anton Chekhov

"But I have been to the doctors already. I could not ring them up."

"H'm . . . you don't regard us chemists as human beings, and disturb our rest even at four o'clock at night, though every dog, every cat, can rest in peace. . . . You don't try to understand anything, and to your thinking we are not people and our nerves are like cords."

Strizhin listened to the chemist, heaved a sigh, and went home.

"So I am fated to die," he thought.

And in his mouth was a burning and a taste of paraffin, there were twinges in his stomach, and a sound of boom, boom, boom in his ears. Every moment it seemed to him that his end was near, that his heart was no longer beating.

Returning home he made haste to write: "Let no one be blamed for my death," then he said his prayers, lay down and pulled the bedclothes over his head. He lay awake till morning expecting death, and all the time he kept fancying how his grave would be covered with fresh green grass and how the birds would twitter over it. . . .

And in the morning he was sitting on his bed, saying with a smile to Dashenka:

"One who leads a steady and regular life, dear sister, is unaffected by any poison. Take me, for example. I have been on the verge of death. I was dying and in agony, yet now I am all right. There is only a burning in my mouth and a soreness in my throat, but I am all right all over, thank God. . . . And why? It's because of my regular life."

"No, it's because it's inferior paraffin!" sighed Dashenka, thinking of the household expenses and gazing into space. "The man at the shop could not have given me the best quality, but that at three farthings. I am a martyr, I am a miserable woman. You monsters! May you suffer the same, in the world to come, accursed Herods. . . ."

And she went on and on. . . .

THE ALBUM

KRATEROV, the titular councillor, as thin and slender as the Admiralty spire, stepped forward and, addressing Zhmyhov, said:

"Your Excellency! Moved and touched to the bottom of our hearts by the way you have ruled us during long years, and by your fatherly care. . . ."

"During the course of more than ten years. . ." Zakusin prompted.

"During the course of more than ten years, we, your subordinates, on this so memorable for us . . . er . . . day, beg your Excellency to accept in token of our respect and profound gratitude this album with our portraits in it, and express our hope that for the duration of your distinguished life, that for long, long years to come, to your dying day you may not abandon us. . . ."

"With your fatherly guidance in the path of justice and progress. . ." added Zakusin, wiping from his brow the perspiration that had suddenly appeared on it; he was evidently longing to speak, and in all probability had a speech ready. "And," he wound up, "may your standard fly for long, long years in the career of genius, industry, and social self-consciousness."

A tear trickled down the wrinkled left cheek of Zhmyhov.

"Gentlemen!" he said in a shaking voice, "I did not expect, I had no idea that you were going to celebrate my modest jubilee. . . . I am touched indeed . . . very much so. . . . I shall not forget this moment to my dying day, and believe me . . . believe me, friends, that no one is so desirous of your welfare as I am . . . and if there has been anything . . . it was for your benefit."

Zhmyhov, the actual civil councillor, kissed the titular councillor Kraterov, who had not expected such an honour, and turned pale with delight. Then the chief made a gesture that signified that he could not speak for emotion, and shed tears as though an expensive album had not been presented to him, but on the contrary, taken from him . . . . Then when he had a little recovered and said a few more words full of feeling and given everyone his hand to shake, he went downstairs amid loud and joyful cheers, got into his carriage and drove off, followed by their blessings. As he sat in his carriage he was aware of a flood of joyous feelings such as he had never known before, and once more he shed tears.

At home new delights awaited him. There his family, his friends, and acquaintances had prepared him such an ovation that it seemed to him that he really had been of very great service to his country, and that if he had never existed his country would perhaps have been in a very bad way. The jubilee dinner was made up of toasts, speeches, and tears. In short, Zhmyhov had never expected that his merits would be so warmly appreciated.

"Gentlemen!" he said before the dessert, "two hours ago I was recompensed for all the sufferings a man has to undergo who is the servant, so to say, not of routine, not of the letter, but of duty! Through the whole duration of my service I have constantly adhered to the principle; - the public does not exist for us, but we for the public, and to-day I received the highest reward! My subordinates presented me with an album . . . see! I was touched."

Festive faces bent over the album and began examining it.

"It's a pretty album," said Zhmyhov's daughter Olya, "it must have cost fifty roubles, I do believe. Oh, it's charming! You must give me the album, papa, do you hear? I'll take care of it, it's so pretty."

After dinner Olya carried off the album to her room and shut it up in her table drawer. Next day she took the clerks out of it, flung them on the floor, and put her school friends in their place. The government uniforms made way for white pelerines. Kolya, his Excellency's little son, picked up the clerks and painted their clothes red. Those who had no moustaches he presented with green moustaches and added brown beards to the beardless. When there was nothing left to paint he cut the little men out of the card-board, pricked their eyes with a pin, and began playing soldiers with them. After cutting out the titular councillor Kraterov, he fixed him on a match-box and carried him in that state to his father's study.

"Papa, a monument, look!"

Zhmyhov burst out laughing, lurched forward, and,

looking tenderly at the child, gave him a warm kiss on the cheek.

"There, you rogue, go and show mamma; let mamma look too."

OH! THE PUBLIC

"HERE goes, I've done with drinking! Nothing. . . n-o-thing shall tempt me to it. It's time to take myself in hand; I must buck up and work. . . You're glad to get your salary, so you must do your work honestly, heartily, conscientiously, regardless of sleep and comfort. Chuck taking it easy. You've got into the way of taking a salary for nothing, my boy - that's not the right thing . . . not the right thing at all. . . ."

After administering to himself several such lectures Podtyagin, the head ticket collector, begins to feel an irresistible impulse to get to work. It is past one o'clock at night, but in spite of that he wakes the ticket collectors and with them goes up and down the railway carriages, inspecting the tickets.

"T-t-t-ickets . . . P-p-p-please!" he keeps shouting, briskly snapping the clippers.

Sleepy figures, shrouded in the twilight of the railway carriages, start, shake their heads, and produce their tickets.

"T-t-t-tickets, please!" Podtyagin addresses a second-class passenger, a lean, scraggy-looking man, wrapped up in a fur coat and a rug and surrounded with pillows. "Tickets, please!"

The scraggy-looking man makes no reply. He is buried in sleep. The head ticket-collector touches him on the shoulder and repeats impatiently: "T-t-tickets, p-p-please!"

The passenger starts, opens his eyes, and gazes in alarm at Podtyagin.

"What? . . . Who? . . . Eh?"

"You're asked in plain language: t-t-tickets, p-p-please! If you please!"

"My God!" moans the scraggy-looking man, pulling a woebegone face. "Good Heavens! I'm suffering from rheumatism. . . . I haven't slept for three nights! I've just taken morphia on purpose to get to sleep, and you . . . with your tickets! It's merciless, it's inhuman! If you knew how hard it is for me to sleep you wouldn't disturb me for such nonsense. . . . It's cruel, it's absurd! And what do you want with my ticket! It's positively stupid!"

Podtyagin considers whether to take offence or not - and decides to take offence.

"Don't shout here! This is not a tavern!"

"No, in a tavern people are more humane. . ." coughs the passenger. "Perhaps you'll let me go to sleep another time! It's extraordinary: I've travelled abroad, all over the place, and no one asked for my ticket there, but here you're at it again and again, as though the devil were after you. . . ."

"Well, you'd better go abroad again since you like it

Anton Chekhov

so much."

"It's stupid, sir! Yes! As though it's not enough killing the passengers with fumes and stuffiness and draughts, they want to strangle us with red tape, too, damn it all! He must have the ticket! My goodness, what zeal! If it were of any use to the company - but half the passengers are travelling without a ticket!"

"Listen, sir!" cries Podtyagin, flaring up. "If you don't leave off shouting and disturbing the public, I shall be obliged to put you out at the next station and to draw up a report on the incident!"

"This is revolting!" exclaims "the public," growing indignant. "Persecuting an invalid! Listen, and have some consideration!"

"But the gentleman himself was abusive!" says Podtyagin, a little scared. "Very well. . . . I won't take the ticket . . . as you like . . . . Only, of course, as you know very well, it's my duty to do so. . . . If it were not my duty, then, of course. . . You can ask the station-master . . . ask anyone you like. . . ."

Podtyagin shrugs his shoulders and walks away from the invalid. At first he feels aggrieved and somewhat injured, then, after passing through two or three carriages, he begins to feel a certain uneasiness not unlike the pricking of conscience in his ticket-collector's bosom.

"There certainly was no need to wake the invalid," he thinks, "though it was not my fault. . . .They imagine I did it wantonly, idly.

They don't know that I'm bound in duty . . . if they don't believe it, I can bring the station-master to them." A station. The train stops five minutes. Before the third bell, Podtyagin enters the same second-class carriage. Behind him stalks the station-master in a red cap.

"This gentleman here," Podtyagin begins, "declares that I have no right to ask for his ticket and . . . and is offended at it. I ask you, Mr. Station-master, to explain to him. . . . Do I ask for tickets according to regulation or to please myself? Sir," Podtyagin addresses the scraggy-looking man, "sir! you can ask the station-master here if you don't believe me."

The invalid starts as though he had been stung, opens his eyes, and with a woebegone face sinks back in his seat.

"My God! I have taken another powder and only just dozed off when here he is again. . . again! I beseech you have some pity on me!"

"You can ask the station-master . . . whether I have the right to demand your ticket or not."

"This is insufferable! Take your ticket. . . take it! I'll pay for five extra if you'll only let me die in peace! Have you never been ill yourself? Heartless people!"

"This is simply persecution!" A gentleman in military uniform grows indignant. "I can see no other explanation of this persistence."

"Drop it . . ." says the station-master, frowning and pulling Podtyagin by the sleeve.

Anton Chekhov

Podtyagin shrugs his shoulders and slowly walks after the station-master.

"There's no pleasing them!" he thinks, bewildered. "It was for his sake I brought the station-master, that he might understand and be pacified, and he . . . swears!"

Another station. The train stops ten minutes. Before the second bell, while Podtyagin is standing at the refreshment bar, drinking seltzer water, two gentlemen go up to him, one in the uniform of an engineer, and the other in a military overcoat.

"Look here, ticket-collector!" the engineer begins, addressing Podtyagin. "Your behaviour to that invalid passenger has revolted all who witnessed it. My name is Puzitsky; I am an engineer, and this gentleman is a colonel. If you do not apologize to the passenger, we shall make a complaint to the traffic manager, who is a friend of ours."

"Gentlemen! Why of course I . . . why of course you . . ." Podtyagin is panic-stricken.

"We don't want explanations. But we warn you, if you don't apologize, we shall see justice done to him."

"Certainly I . . . I'll apologize, of course. . . To be sure. . . ."

Half an hour later, Podtyagin having thought of an apologetic phrase which would satisfy the passenger without lowering his own dignity, walks into the carriage. "Sir," he addresses the invalid. "Listen, sir. . . ."

The invalid starts and leaps up: "What?"

"I . . . what was it? . . . You mustn't be offended. . . ."

"Och! Water . . ." gasps the invalid, clutching at his heart. "I'd just taken a third dose of morphia, dropped asleep, and . . . again! Good God! when will this torture cease!"

"I only . . . you must excuse . . ."

"Oh! . . . Put me out at the next station! I can't stand any more . . . . I . . . I am dying. . . ."

"This is mean, disgusting!" cry the "public," revolted. "Go away! You shall pay for such persecution. Get away!"

Podtyagin waves his hand in despair, sighs, and walks out of the carriage. He goes to the attendants' compartment, sits down at the table, exhausted, and complains:

"Oh, the public! There's no satisfying them! It's no use working and doing one's best! One's driven to drinking and cursing it all . . . . If you do nothing - they're angry; if you begin doing your duty, they're angry too. There's nothing for it but drink!"

Podtyagin empties a bottle straight off and thinks no more of work, duty, and honesty!

A TRIPPING TONGUE

NATALYA MIHALOVNA, a young married lady who had arrived in the morning from Yalta, was having her dinner, and in a never-ceasing flow of babble was telling her husband of all the charms of the Crimea. Her husband, delighted, gazed tenderly at her enthusiastic face, listened, and from time to time put in a question.

"But they say living is dreadfully expensive there?" he asked, among other things.

"Well, what shall I say? To my thinking this talk of its being so expensive is exaggerated, hubby. The devil is not as black as he is painted. Yulia Petrovna and I, for instance, had very decent and comfortable rooms for twenty roubles a day. Everything depends on knowing how to do things, my dear. Of course if you want to go up into the mountains . . . to Aie-Petri for instance . . . if you take a horse, a guide, then of course it does come to something. It's awful what it comes to! But, Vassitchka, the mountains there! Imagine high, high mountains, a thousand times higher than the church. . . . At the top - mist, mist, mist. . . . At the bottom - enormous stones, stones, stones. . . . And pines. . . . Ah, I can't bear to think of it!"

"By the way, I read about those Tatar guides there, in

some magazine while you were away . . . . such abominable stories! Tell me is there really anything out of the way about them?"

Natalya Mihalovna made a little disdainful grimace and shook her head.

"Just ordinary Tatars, nothing special . . ." she said, "though indeed I only had a glimpse of them in the distance. They were pointed out to me, but I did not take much notice of them. You know, hubby, I always had a prejudice against all such Circassians, Greeks . . . Moors!"

"They are said to be terrible Don Juans."

"Perhaps! There are shameless creatures who . . . ."

Natalya Mihalovna suddenly jumped up from her chair, as though she had thought of something dreadful; for half a minute she looked with frightened eyes at her husband and said, accentuating each word:

"Vassitchka, I say, the im-mo-ral women there are in the world! Ah, how immoral! And it's not as though they were working-class or middle-class people, but aristocratic ladies, priding themselves on their *bon-ton!* It was simply awful, I could not believe my own eyes! I shall remember it as long as I live! To think that people can forget themselves to such a point as . . . ach, Vassitchka, I don't like to speak of it! Take my companion, Yulia Petrovna, for example. . . . Such a good husband, two children . . . she moves in a decent circle, always poses as a saint - and all at once, would you believe it. . . . Only, hubby, of course this is *entre nous*. . . . Give me your word of honour you won't tell a soul?"

"What next! Of course I won't tell."

"Honour bright? Mind now! I trust you. . . ."

The little lady put down her fork, assumed a mysterious air, and whispered:

"Imagine a thing like this. . . . That Yulia Petrovna rode up into the mountains . . . . It was glorious weather! She rode on ahead with her guide, I was a little behind. We had ridden two or three miles, all at once, only fancy, Vassitchka, Yulia cried out and clutched at her bosom. Her Tatar put his arm round her waist or she would have fallen off the saddle. . . . I rode up to her with my guide. . . . 'What is it? What is the matter?' 'Oh,' she cried, 'I am dying! I feel faint! I can't go any further' Fancy my alarm! 'Let us go back then,' I said. 'No, *Natalie*,' she said, 'I can't go back! I shall die of pain if I move another step! I have spasms.' And she prayed and besought my Suleiman and me to ride back to the town and fetch her some of her drops which always do her good."

"Stay. . . . I don't quite understand you," muttered the husband, scratching his forehead. "You said just now that you had only seen those Tatars from a distance, and now you are talking of some Suleiman."

"There, you are finding fault again," the lady pouted, not in the least disconcerted. "I can't endure suspicio-usness! I can't endure it! It's stupid, stupid!"

"I am not finding fault, but . . . why say what is not true? If you rode about with Tatars, so be it, God bless you, but . . . why shuffle about it?"

"H'm! . . . you are a queer one!" cried the lady, revolted. "He is jealous of Suleiman! as though one could ride up into the mountains without a guide! I should like to see you do it! If you don't know the ways there, if you don't understand, you had better hold your tongue! Yes, hold your tongue. You can't take a step there without a guide."

"So it seems!"

"None of your silly grins, if you please! I am not a Yulia. . . . I don't justify her but I . . . ! Though I don't pose as a saint, I don't forget myself to that degree. My Suleiman never overstepped the limits. . . . No-o! Mametkul used to be sitting at Yulia's all day long, but in my room as soon as it struck eleven: 'Suleiman, march! Off you go!' And my foolish Tatar boy would depart. I made him mind his p's and q's, hubby! As soon as he began grumbling about money or anything, I would say 'How? Wha-at? Wha-a-a-t?' And his heart would be in his mouth directly. . . . Ha-ha-ha! His eyes, you know, Vassitchka, were as black, as black, like coals, such an amusing little Tatar face, so funny and silly! I kept him in order, didn't I just!"

"I can fancy . . ." mumbled her husband, rolling up pellets of bread.

"That's stupid, Vassitchka! I know what is in your mind! I know what you are thinking . . . But I assure you even when we were on our expeditions I never let him overstep the limits. For instance, if we rode to the mountains or to the U-Chan-Su waterfall, I would always say to him, 'Suleiman, ride behind! Do you hear!' And he always rode behind, poor boy. . . . Even when we . . . even at the most dramatic moments I would say to him, 'Still, you must not forget that you are only a Tatar and I am the wife of a civil councillor!' Ha-ha. . . ."

The little lady laughed, then, looking round her quickly and assuming an alarmed expression, whispered:

"But Yulia! Oh, that Yulia! I quite see, Vassitchka, there is no reason why one shouldn't have a little fun, a little rest from the emptiness of conventional life! That's all right, have your fling by all means - no one will blame you, but to take the thing seriously, to get up scenes . . . no, say what you like, I cannot understand that! Just fancy, she was jealous! Wasn't that silly? One day Mametkul, her *grande passion*, came to see her . . . she was not at home. . . . Well, I asked him into my room . . . there was conversation, one thing and another . . . they're awfully amusing, you know! The evening passed without our noticing it. . . . All at once Yulia rushed in. . . . She flew at me and at Mametkul - made such a scene . . . fi! I can't understand that sort of thing, Vassitchka."

Vassitchka cleared his throat, frowned, and walked up and down the room.

"You had a gay time there, I must say," he growled with a disdainful smile.

"How stu-upid that is!" cried Natalya Mihalovna, offended. "I know what you are thinking about! You always have such horrid ideas! I won't tell you anything! No, I won't!"

The lady pouted and said no more.

Anton Chekhov

OVERDOING IT

GLYEB GAVRILOVITCH SMIRNOV, a land surveyor, arrived at the station of Gnilushki. He had another twenty or thirty miles to drive before he would reach the estate which he had been summoned to survey. (If the driver were not drunk and the horses were not bad, it would hardly be twenty miles, but if the driver had had a drop and his steeds were worn out it would mount up to a good forty.)

"Tell me, please, where can I get post-horses here?" the surveyor asked of the station gendarme.

"What? Post-horses? There's no finding a decent dog for seventy miles round, let alone post-horses. . . . But where do you want to go?"

"To Dyevkino, General Hohotov's estate."

"Well," yawned the gendarme, "go outside the station, there are sometimes peasants in the yard there, they will take passengers."

The surveyor heaved a sigh and made his way out of the station.

There, after prolonged enquiries, conversations, and hesitations, he found a very sturdy, sullen-looking pock-marked peasant, wearing a tattered grey smock and bark-shoes.

"You have got a queer sort of cart!" said the surveyor, frowning as he clambered into the cart. "There is no making out which is the back and which is the front."

"What is there to make out? Where the horse's tail is, there's the front, and where your honour's sitting, there's the back."

The little mare was young, but thin, with legs planted wide apart and frayed ears. When the driver stood up and lashed her with a whip made of cord, she merely shook her head; when he swore at her and lashed her once more, the cart squeaked and shivered as though in a fever. After the third lash the cart gave a lurch, after the fourth, it moved forward.

"Are we going to drive like this all the way?" asked the surveyor, violently jolted and marvelling at the capacity of Russian drivers for combining a slow tortoise-like pace with a jolting that turns the soul inside out.

"We shall ge-et there!" the peasant reassured him. "The mare is young and frisky. . . . Only let her get running and then there is no stopping her. . . . No-ow, cur-sed brute!"

It was dusk by the time the cart drove out of the station. On the surveyor's right hand stretched a dark frozen plain, endless and boundless. If you drove over it you would certainly get to the other side of beyond. On the horizon, where it vanished and melted into the sky, there was the languid glow of a cold autumn

Anton Chekhov

sunset. . . . On the left of the road, mounds of some sort, that might be last year's stacks or might be a village, rose up in the gathering darkness. The surveyor could not see what was in front as his whole field of vision on that side was covered by the broad clumsy back of the driver. The air was still, but it was cold and frosty.

"What a wilderness it is here," thought the surveyor, trying to cover his ears with the collar of his overcoat. "Neither post nor paddock. If, by ill-luck, one were attacked and robbed no one would hear you, whatever uproar you made. . . . And the driver is not one you could depend on. . . . Ugh, what a huge back! A child of nature like that has only to move a finger and it would be all up with one! And his ugly face is suspicious and brutal-looking."

"Hey, my good man!" said the surveyor, "What is your name?"

"Mine? Klim."

"Well, Klim, what is it like in your parts here? Not dangerous? Any robbers on the road?"

"It is all right, the Lord has spared us. . . . Who should go robbing on the road?"

"It's a good thing there are no robbers. But to be ready for anything I have got three revolvers with me," said the surveyor untruthfully. "And it doesn't do to trifle with a revolver, you know. One can manage a dozen robbers. . . ."

It had become quite dark. The cart suddenly began

creaking, squeaking, shaking, and, as though unwillingly, turned sharply to the left.

"Where is he taking me to?" the surveyor wondered. "He has been driving straight and now all at once to the left. I shouldn't wonder if he'll take me, the rascal, to some den of thieves . . . and. . . . Things like that do happen."

"I say," he said, addressing the driver, "so you tell me it's not dangerous here? That's a pity. . . I like a fight with robbers. . . . I am thin and sickly-looking, but I have the strength of a bull . . . . Once three robbers attacked me and what do you think? I gave one such a dressing that. . . that he gave up his soul to God, you understand, and the other two were sent to penal servitude in Siberia. And where I got the strength I can't say. . . . One grips a strapping fellow of your sort with one hand and . . . wipes him out."

Klim looked round at the surveyor, wrinkled up his whole face, and lashed his horse.

"Yes . . ." the surveyor went on. "God forbid anyone should tackle me. The robber would have his bones broken, and, what's more, he would have to answer for it in the police court too. . . . I know all the judges and the police captains, I am a man in the Government, a man of importance. Here I am travelling and the authorities know . . . they keep a regular watch over me to see no one does me a mischief. There are policemen and village constables stuck behind bushes all along the road. . . . Sto . . . sto . . . . stop!" the surveyor bawled suddenly. "Where have you got to? Where are you taking me to?"

Anton Chekhov

"Why, don't you see? It's a forest!"

"It certainly is a forest," thought the surveyor. "I was frightened! But it won't do to betray my feelings. . . . He has noticed already that I am in a funk. Why is it he has taken to looking round at me so often? He is plotting something for certain. . . . At first he drove like a snail and now how he is dashing along!"

"I say, Klim, why are you making the horse go like that?"

"I am not making her go. She is racing along of herself. . . . Once she gets into a run there is no means of stopping her. It's no pleasure to her that her legs are like that."

"You are lying, my man, I see that you are lying. Only I advise you not to drive so fast. Hold your horse in a bit. . . . Do you hear? Hold her in!"

"What for?"

"Why . . . why, because four comrades were to drive after me from the station. We must let them catch us up. . . . They promised to overtake us in this forest. It will be more cheerful in their company. . . . They are a strong, sturdy set of fellows. . . . And each of them has got a pistol. Why do you keep looking round and fidgeting as though you were sitting on thorns? eh? I, my good fellow, er . . . my good fellow . . . there is no need to look around at me . . . there is nothing interesting about me. . . . Except perhaps the revolvers. Well, if you like I will take them out and show you. . . ."

The surveyor made a pretence of feeling in his pockets and at that moment something happened which he could not have expected with all his cowardice. Klim suddenly rolled off the cart and ran as fast as he could go into the forest.

"Help!" he roared. "Help! Take the horse and the cart, you devil, only don't take my life. Help!"

There was the sound of footsteps hurriedly retreating, of twigs snapping - and all was still. . . . The surveyor had not expected such a *denouement*. He first stopped the horse and then settled himself more comfortably in the cart and fell to thinking.

"He has run off . . . he was scared, the fool. Well, what's to be done now? I can't go on alone because I don't know the way; besides they may think I have stolen his horse. . . . What's to be done?"

"Klim! Klim," he cried.

"Klim," answered the echo.

At the thought that he would have to sit through the whole night in the cold and dark forest and hear nothing but the wolves, the echo, and the snorting of the scraggy mare, the surveyor began to have twinges down his spine as though it were being rasped with a cold file.

"Klimushka," he shouted. "Dear fellow! Where are you, Klimushka?"

For two hours the surveyor shouted, and it was only after he was quite husky and had resigned himself to

Anton Chekhov

spending the night in the forest that a faint breeze wafted the sound of a moan to him.

"Klim, is it you, dear fellow? Let us go on."

"You'll mu-ur-der me!"

"But I was joking, my dear man! I swear to God I was joking! As though I had revolvers! I told a lie because I was frightened. For goodness sake let us go on, I am freezing!"

Klim, probably reflecting that a real robber would have vanished long ago with the horse and cart, came out of the forest and went hesitatingly up to his passenger.

"Well, what were you frightened of, stupid? I . . . I was joking and you were frightened. Get in!"

"God be with you, sir," Klim muttered as he clambered into the cart, "if I had known I wouldn't have taken you for a hundred roubles. I almost died of fright. . . ."

Klim lashed at the little mare. The cart swayed. Klim lashed once more and the cart gave a lurch. After the fourth stroke of the whip when the cart moved forward, the surveyor hid his ears in his collar and sank into thought.

The road and Klim no longer seemed dangerous to him.

THE ORATOR

ONE fine morning the collegiate assessor, Kirill Ivanovitch Babilonov, who had died of the two afflictions so widely spread in our country, a bad wife and alcoholism, was being buried. As the funeral procession set off from the church to the cemetery, one of the deceased's colleagues, called Poplavsky, got into a cab and galloped off to find a friend, one Grigory Petrovitch Zapoikin, a man who though still young had acquired considerable popularity. Zapoikin, as many of my readers are aware, possesses a rare talent for impromptu speechifying at weddings, jubilees, and funerals. He can speak whenever he likes: in his sleep, on an empty stomach, dead drunk or in a high fever. His words flow smoothly and evenly, like water out of a pipe, and in abundance; there are far more moving words in his oratorical dictionary than there are beetles in any restaurant. He always speaks eloquently and at great length, so much so that on some occasions, particularly at merchants' weddings, they have to resort to assistance from the police to stop him.

"I have come for you, old man!" began Poplavsky, finding him at home. "Put on your hat and coat this minute and come along. One of our fellows is dead, we are just sending him off to the other world, so you must do a bit of palavering by way of farewell to him. . . . You are our only hope. If it had been one of the smaller fry it would not have been worth troubling you, but you see it's the secretary . . . a pillar of the office, in a sense. It's awkward for such a whopper to be buried without a speech."

"Oh, the secretary!" yawned Zapoikin. "You mean the drunken one?"

"Yes. There will be pancakes, a lunch . . . you'll get your cab-fare. Come along, dear chap. You spout out some rigmarole like a regular Cicero at the grave and what gratitude you will earn!"

Zapoikin readily agreed. He ruffled up his hair, cast a shade of melancholy over his face, and went out into the street with Poplavsky.

"I know your secretary," he said, as he got into the cab. "A cunning rogue and a beast - the kingdom of heaven be his - such as you don't often come across."

"Come, Grisha, it is not the thing to abuse the dead."

"Of course not, *aut mortuis nihil bene*, but still he was a rascal."

The friends overtook the funeral procession and joined it. The coffin was borne along slowly so that before they reached the cemetery they were able three times to drop into a tavern and imbibe a little to the health of the departed.

In the cemetery came the service by the graveside. The mother-in-law, the wife, and the sister-in-law in obedience to custom shed many tears. When the coffin was being lowered into the grave the wife even shrieked "Let me go with him!" but did not follow her husband into the grave probably recollecting her pension. Waiting till everything was quiet again Zapoikin stepped forward, turned his eyes on all present, and began:

"Can I believe my eyes and ears? Is it not a terrible dream this grave, these tear-stained faces, these moans and lamentations? Alas, it is not a dream and our eyes do not deceive us! He whom we have only so lately seen, so full of courage, so youthfully fresh and pure, who so lately before our eyes like an unwearying bee bore his honey to the common hive of the welfare of the state, he who . . . he is turned now to dust, to inanimate mirage. Inexorable death has laid his bony hand upon him at the time when, in spite of his bowed age, he was still full of the bloom of strength and radiant hopes. An irremediable loss! Who will fill his place for us? Good government servants we have many, but Prokofy Osipitch was unique. To the depths of his soul he was devoted to his honest duty; he did not spare his strength but worked late at night, and was disinterested, impervious to bribes. . . . How he despised those who to the detriment of the public interest sought to corrupt him, who by the seductive goods of this life strove to draw him to betray his duty! Yes, before our eyes Prokofy Osipitch would divide his small salary between his poorer colleagues, and you have just heard yourselves the lamentations of the widows and orphans who lived upon his alms. Devoted to good works and his official duty, he gave up the joys of this life and even renounced the happiness of domestic existence; as you are aware, to the end of his days he was a bachelor. And who will replace him as a comrade? I can see now the kindly, shaven face turned to us with a gentle smile, I can hear now his soft friendly voice. Peace to thine ashes, Prokofy Osipitch! Rest, honest, noble toiler!"

Zapoikin continued while his listeners began whispering together. His speech pleased everyone and drew some tears, but a good many things in it seemed strange. In the first place they could not make out why the orator called the deceased Prokofy Osipitch when his name was Kirill Ivanovitch. In the second, everyone knew that the deceased had spent his whole life quarelling with his lawful wife, and so consequently could not be called a bachelor; in the third, he had a thick red beard and had never been known to shave, and so no one could understand why the orator spoke of his shaven face. The listeners were perplexed; they glanced at each other and shrugged their shoulders.

"Prokofy Osipitch," continued the orator, looking with an air of inspiration into the grave, "your face was plain, even hideous, you were morose and austere, but we all know that under that outer husk there beat an honest, friendly heart!"

Soon the listeners began to observe something strange in the orator himself. He gazed at one point, shifted about uneasily and began to shrug his shoulders too. All at once he ceased speaking, and gaping with astonishment, turned to Poplavsky.

"I say! he's alive," he said, staring with horror.

"Who's alive?"

"Why, Prokofy Osipitch, there he stands, by that tombstone!"

"He never died! It's Kirill Ivanovitch who's dead."

"But you told me yourself your secretary was dead."

"Kirill Ivanovitch was our secretary. You've muddled it, you queer fish. Prokofy Osipitch was our secretary before, that's true, but two years ago he was transferred to the second division as head clerk."

"How the devil is one to tell?"

"Why are you stopping? Go on, it's awkward."

Zapoikin turned to the grave, and with the same eloquence continued his interrupted speech. Prokofy Osipitch, an old clerk with a clean-shaven face, was in fact standing by a tombstone. He looked at the orator and frowned angrily.

"Well, you have put your foot into it, haven't you!" laughed his fellow-clerks as they returned from the funeral with Zapoikin. "Burying a man alive!"

"It's unpleasant, young man," grumbled Prokofy Osipitch. "Your speech may be all right for a dead man, but in reference to a living one it is nothing but sarcasm! Upon my soul what have you been saying? Disinterested, incorruptible, won't take bribes! Such things can only be said of the living in sarcasm. And no one asked you, sir, to expatiate on my face. Plain, hideous, so be it, but why exhibit my countenance in that public way! It's insulting."

MALINGERERS

MARFA PETROVNA PETCHONKIN, the General's widow, who has been practising for ten years as a homeopathic doctor, is seeing patients in her study on one of the Tuesdays in May. On the table before her lie a chest of homeopathic drugs, a book on homeopathy, and bills from a homeopathic chemist. On the wall the letters from some Petersburg homeopath, in Marfa Petrovna's opinion a very celebrated and great man, hang under glass in a gilt frame, and there also is a portrait of Father Aristark, to whom the lady owes her salvation - that is, the renunciation of pernicious allopathy and the knowledge of the truth. In the vestibule patients are sitting waiting, for the most part peasants. All but two or three of them are barefoot, as the lady has given orders that their ill-smelling boots are to be left in the yard.

Marfa Petrovna has already seen ten patients when she calls the eleventh: "Gavrila Gruzd!"

The door opens and instead of Gavrila Gruzd, Zamuhrishen, a neighbouring landowner who has sunk into poverty, a little old man with sour eyes, and with a gentleman's cap under his arm, walks into the room. He puts down his stick in the corner, goes up to the lady, and without a word drops on one knee before her.

"What are you about, Kuzma Kuzmitch?" cries the lady in horror, flushing crimson. "For goodness sake!"

"While I live I will not rise," says Zamuhrishen, bending over her hand. "Let all the world see my homage on my knees, our guardian angel, benefactress of the human race! Let them! Before the good fairy who has given me life, guided me into the path of truth, and enlightened my scepticism I am ready not merely to kneel but to pass through fire, our miraculous healer, mother of the orphan and the widowed! I have recovered. I am a new man, enchantress!"

"I . . . I am very glad . . ." mutters the lady, flushing with pleasure. "It's so pleasant to hear that. . . Sit down please! Why, you were so seriously ill that Tuesday."

"Yes indeed, how ill I was! It's awful to recall it," says Zamuhrishen, taking a seat. "I had rheumatism in every part and every organ. I have been in misery for eight years, I've had no rest from it . . . by day or by night, my benefactress. I have consulted doctors, and I went to professors at Kazan; I have tried all sorts of mud-baths, and drunk waters, and goodness knows what I haven't tried! I have wasted all my substance on doctors, my beautiful lady. The doctors did me nothing but harm. They drove the disease inwards. Drive in, that they did, but to drive out was beyond their science. All they care about is their fees, the brigands; but as for the benefit of humanity - for that they don't care a straw. They prescribe some quackery, and you have to drink it. Assassins, that's the only word for them. If it hadn't been for you, our angel, I should have been in the grave by now! I went home from you that Tuesday, looked at the pilules that you gave me then, and wondered what good there could be in them. Was it possible that those little grains, scarcely visible, could cure my immense, long-standing disease? That's what I thought - unbeliever that I was! - and I smiled; but when I took the pilule - it was instantaneous! It was as though I had not been ill, or as though it had been lifted off me. My wife looked at me with her eyes starting out of her head and couldn't believe it. 'Why, is it you, Kolya?' 'Yes, it is I,' I said. And we knelt down together before the ikon, and fell to praying for our angel: 'Send her, O Lord, all that we are feeling!'"

Zamuhrishen wipes his eyes with his sleeve gets up from his chair, and shows a disposition to drop on one knee again; but the lady checks him and makes him sit down.

"It's not me you must thank," she says, blushing with excitement and looking enthusiastically at the portrait of Father Aristark. "It's not my doing. . . . I am only the obedient instrument . . It's really a miracle. Rheumatism of eight years' standing by one pilule of scrofuloso!"

"Excuse me, you were so kind as to give me three pilules. One I took at dinner and the effect was instantaneous! Another in the evening, and the third next day; and since then not a touch! Not a twinge anywhere! And you know I thought I was dying, I had written to Moscow for my son to come! The Lord has given you wisdom, our lady of healing! Now I am walking, and feel as though I were in Paradise. The Tuesday I came to you I was hobbling, and now I am ready to run after a hare. . . . I could live for a hundred years. There's only one trouble, our lack of means. I'm well now, but what's the use of health if there's nothing

to live on? Poverty weighs on me worse than illness
. . . . For example, take this . . . It's the time to sow
oats, and how is one to sow it if one has no seed? I
ought to buy it, but the money . . . everyone knows
how we are off for money. . . ."

"I will give you oats, Kuzma Kuzmitch. . . . Sit down,
sit down. You have so delighted me, you have given
me so much pleasure that it's not you but I that should
say thank you!"

"You are our joy! That the Lord should create such
goodness! Rejoice, Madam, looking at your good
deeds! . . . While we sinners have no cause for
rejoicing in ourselves. . . . We are paltry, poor-spirited,
useless people . . . a mean lot. . . . We are only gentry
in name, but in a material sense we are the same as
peasants, only worse. . . . We live in stone houses, but
it's a mere make-believe . . . for the roof leaks. And
there is no money to buy wood to mend it with."

"I'll give you the wood, Kuzma Kuzmitch."

Zamuhrishen asks for and gets a cow too, a letter of
recommendation for his daughter whom he wants to
send to a boarding school, and . . . touched by the
lady's liberality he whimpers with excess of feeling,
twists his mouth, and feels in his pocket for his
handkerchief . . . .

Marfa Petrovna sees a red paper slip out of his pocket
with his handkerchief and fall noiselessly to the floor.

"I shall never forget it to all eternity . . ." he mutters,
"and I shall make my children and my grandchildren
remember it . . . from generation to generation. 'See,

children,' I shall say, 'who has saved me from the grave, who . . .'"

When she has seen her patient out, the lady looks for a minute at Father Aristark with eyes full of tears, then turns her caressing, reverent gaze on the drug chest, the books, the bills, the armchair in which the man she had saved from death has just been sitting, and her eyes fall on the paper just dropped by her patient. She picks up the paper, unfolds it, and sees in it three pilules - the very pilules she had given Zamuhrishen the previous Tuesday.

"They are the very ones," she thinks puzzled. ". . . The paper is the same. . . . He hasn't even unwrapped them! What has he taken then? Strange. . . . Surely he wouldn't try to deceive me!"

And for the first time in her ten years of practice a doubt creeps into Marfa Petrovna's mind. . . . She summons the other patients, and while talking to them of their complaints notices what has hitherto slipped by her ears unnoticed. The patients, every one of them as though they were in a conspiracy, first belaud her for their miraculous cure, go into raptures over her medical skill, and abuse allopath doctors, then when she is flushed with excitement, begin holding forth on their needs. One asks for a bit of land to plough, another for wood, a third for permission to shoot in her forests, and so on. She looks at the broad, benevolent countenance of Father Aristark who has revealed the truth to her, and a new truth begins gnawing at her heart. An evil oppressive truth. . . .

The deceitfulness of man!

IN THE GRAVEYARD

"THE wind has got up, friends, and it is beginning to get dark. Hadn't we better take ourselves off before it gets worse?"

The wind was frolicking among the yellow leaves of the old birch trees, and a shower of thick drops fell upon us from the leaves. One of our party slipped on the clayey soil, and clutched at a big grey cross to save himself from falling.

"Yegor Gryaznorukov, titular councillor and cavalier . ." he read. "I knew that gentleman. He was fond of his wife, he wore the Stanislav ribbon, and read nothing. . . . His digestion worked well . . . . life was all right, wasn't it? One would have thought he had no reason to die, but alas! fate had its eye on him. . . . The poor fellow fell a victim to his habits of observation. On one occasion, when he was listening at a keyhole, he got such a bang on the head from the door that he sustained concussion of the brain (he had a brain), and died. And here, under this tombstone, lies a man who from his cradle detested verses and epigrams. . . . As though to mock him his whole tombstone is adorned with verses. . . . There is someone coming!"

A man in a shabby overcoat, with a shaven, bluish-crimson countenance, overtook us. He had a bottle under his arm and a parcel of sausage was sticking out of his pocket.

"Where is the grave of Mushkin, the actor?" he asked us in a husky voice.

We conducted him towards the grave of Mushkin, the actor, who had died two years before.

"You are a government clerk, I suppose?" we asked him.

"No, an actor. Nowadays it is difficult to distinguish actors from clerks of the Consistory. No doubt you have noticed that. . . . That's typical, but it's not very flattering for the government clerk."

It was with difficulty that we found the actor's grave. It had sunken, was overgrown with weeds, and had lost all appearance of a grave. A cheap, little cross that had begun to rot, and was covered with green moss blackened by the frost, had an air of aged dejection and looked, as it were, ailing.

". . . forgotten friend Mushkin . . ." we read.

Time had erased the *never*, and corrected the falsehood of man.

"A subscription for a monument to him was got up among actors and journalists, but they drank up the money, the dear fellows . . ." sighed the actor, bowing down to the ground and touching the wet earth with his knees and his cap.

"How do you mean, drank it?"

That's very simple. They collected the money, published a paragraph about it in the newspaper, and spent it on drink. . . . I don't say it to blame them. . . . I hope it did them good, dear things! Good health to them, and eternal memory to him."

"Drinking means bad health, and eternal memory nothing but sadness. God give us remembrance for a time, but eternal memory - what next!"

"You are right there. Mushkin was a well-known man, you see; there were a dozen wreaths on the coffin, and he is already forgotten. Those to whom he was dear have forgotten him, but those to whom he did harm remember him. I, for instance, shall never, never forget him, for I got nothing but harm from him. I have no love for the deceased."

"What harm did he do you?"

"Great harm," sighed the actor, and an expression of bitter resentment overspread his face. "To me he was a villain and a scoundrel - the Kingdom of Heaven be his! It was through looking at him and listening to him that I became an actor. By his art he lured me from the parental home, he enticed me with the excitements of an actor's life, promised me all sorts of things - and brought tears and sorrow. . . . An actor's lot is a bitter one! I have lost youth, sobriety, and the divine semblance. . . . I haven't a half-penny to bless myself with, my shoes are down at heel, my breeches are frayed and patched, and my face looks as if it had been gnawed by dogs. . . . My head's full of freethinking and nonsense. . . . He robbed me of my faith - my evil genius! It would have been something if I had had talent, but as it is, I am ruined for nothing. . . . It's cold, honoured friends. . . . Won't you have some? There is enough for all. . . . B-r-r-r. . . . Let us drink to the rest of his soul! Though I don't like him and though he's dead, he was the only one I had in the world, the only one. It's the last time I shall visit him. . . . The doctors say I shall soon die of drink, so here I have come to say good-bye. One must forgive one's enemies."

We left the actor to converse with the dead Mushkin and went on. It began drizzling a fine cold rain.

At the turning into the principal avenue strewn with gravel, we met a funeral procession. Four bearers, wearing white calico sashes and muddy high boots with leaves sticking on them, carried the brown coffin. It was getting dark and they hastened, stumbling and shaking their burden. . . .

"We've only been walking here for a couple of hours and that is the third brought in already. . . . Shall we go home, friends?"

HUSH!

IVAN YEGORITCH KRASNYHIN, a fourth-rate journalist, returns home late at night, grave and care-worn, with a peculiar air of concentration. He looks like a man expecting a police-raid or contemplating suicide. Pacing about his rooms he halts abruptly, ruffles up his hair, and says in the tone in which Laertes announces his intention of avenging his sister:

"Shattered, soul-weary, a sick load of misery on the heart . . . and then to sit down and write. And this is called life! How is it nobody has described the agonizing discord in the soul of a writer who has to amuse the crowd when his heart is heavy or to shed tears at the word of command when his heart is light? I must be playful, coldly unconcerned, witty, but what if I am weighed down with misery, what if I am ill, or my child is dying or my wife in anguish!"

He says this, brandishing his fists and rolling his eyes. . . . Then he goes into the bedroom and wakes his wife.

"Nadya," he says, "I am sitting down to write. . . . Please don't let anyone interrupt me. I can't write with children crying or cooks snoring. . . . See, too, that there's tea and . . . steak or something. . . . You know that I can't write without tea. . . . Tea is the one thing that gives me the energy for my work."

Returning to his room he takes off his coat, waistcoat, and boots. He does this very slowly; then, assuming an expression of injured innocence, he sits down to his table.

There is nothing casual, nothing ordinary on his writing-table, down to the veriest trifle everything bears the stamp of a stern, deliberately planned programme. Little busts and photographs of distinguished writers, heaps of rough manuscripts, a volume of Byelinsky with a page turned down, part of a skull by way of an ash-tray, a sheet of newspaper folded carelessly, but so that a passage is uppermost, boldly marked in blue pencil with the word "disgraceful." There are a dozen sharply-pointed pencils and several penholders fitted with new nibs, put in readiness that no accidental breaking of a pen may for a single second interrupt the flight of his creative fancy.

Ivan Yegoritch throws himself back in his chair, and closing his eyes concentrates himself on his subject. He hears his wife shuffling about in her slippers and splitting shavings to heat the samovar. She is hardly awake, that is apparent from the way the knife and the lid of the samovar keep dropping from her hands. Soon the hissing of the samovar and the spluttering of the frying meat reaches him. His wife is still splitting shavings and rattling with the doors and blowers of the stove.

All at once Ivan Yegoritch starts, opens frightened eyes, and begins to sniff the air.

"Heavens! the stove is smoking!" he groans, grimacing

with a face of agony. "Smoking! That insufferable woman makes a point of trying to poison me! How, in God's Name, am I to write in such surroundings, kindly tell me that?"

He rushes into the kitchen and breaks into a theatrical wail. When a little later, his wife, stepping cautiously on tiptoe, brings him in a glass of tea, he is sitting in an easy chair as before with his eyes closed, absorbed in his article. He does not stir, drums lightly on his forehead with two fingers, and pretends he is not aware of his wife's presence. . . . His face wears an expression of injured innocence.

Like a girl who has been presented with a costly fan, he spends a long time coquetting, grimacing, and posing to himself before he writes the title. . . . He presses his temples, he wriggles, and draws his legs up under his chair as though he were in pain, or half closes his eyes languidly like a cat on the sofa. At last, not without hesitation, he stretches out his hand towards the inkstand, and with an expression as though he were signing a death-warrant, writes the title. . . .

"Mammy, give me some water!" he hears his son's voice.

"Hush!" says his mother. "Daddy's writing! Hush!"

Daddy writes very, very quickly, without corrections or pauses, he has scarcely time to turn over the pages. The busts and portraits of celebrated authors look at his swiftly racing pen and, keeping stock still, seem to be thinking: "Oh my, how you are going it!"

"Sh!" squeaks the pen.

"Sh!" whisper the authors, when his knee jolts the table and they are set trembling.

All at once Krasnyhin draws himself up, lays down his pen and listens. . . . He hears an even monotonous whispering. . . . It is Foma Nikolaevitch, the lodger in the next room, saying his prayers.

"I say!" cries Krasnyhin. "Couldn't you, please, say your prayers more quietly? You prevent me from writing!"

"Very sorry. . . ." Foma Nikolaevitch answers timidly.

After covering five pages, Krasnyhin stretches and looks at his watch.

"Goodness, three o'clock already," he moans. "Other people are asleep while I . . . I alone must work!"

Shattered and exhausted he goes, with his head on one side, to the bedroom to wake his wife, and says in a languid voice:

"Nadya, get me some more tea! I . . . feel weak."

He writes till four o'clock and would readily have written till six if his subject had not been exhausted. Coquetting and posing to himself and the inanimate objects about him, far from any indiscreet, critical eye, tyrannizing and domineering over the little anthill that fate has put in his power are the honey and the salt of his existence. And how different is this despot here at home from the humble, meek, dull-witted little man we are accustomed to see in the editor's offices!

"I am so exhausted that I am afraid I shan't sleep . . ." he says as he gets into bed. "Our work, this cursed, ungrateful hard labour, exhausts the soul even more than the body. . . . I had better take some bromide. . . . God knows, if it were not for my family I'd throw up the work. . . . To write to order! It is awful."

He sleeps till twelve or one o'clock in the day, sleeps a sound, healthy sleep. . . . Ah! how he would sleep, what dreams he would have, how he would spread himself if he were to become a well-known writer, an editor, or even a sub-editor!

"He has been writing all night," whispers his wife with a scared expression on her face. "Sh!"

No one dares to speak or move or make a sound. His sleep is something sacred, and the culprit who offends against it will pay dearly for his fault.

"Hush!" floats over the flat. "Hush!"

IN AN HOTEL

"LET me tell you, my good man," began Madame Nashatyrin, the colonel's lady at No. 47, crimson and spluttering, as she pounced on the hotel-keeper. "Either give me other apartments, or I shall leave your confounded hotel altogether! It's a sink of iniquity! Mercy on us, I have grown-up daughters and one hears nothing but abominations day and night! It's beyond everything! Day and night! Sometimes he fires off such things that it simply makes one's ears blush! Positively like a cabman. It's a good thing that my poor girls don't understand or I should have to fly out into the street with them. . . He's saying something now! You listen!"

"I know a thing better than that, my boy," a husky bass floated in from the next room. "Do you remember Lieutenant Druzhkov? Well, that same Druzhkov was one day making a drive with the yellow into the pocket and as he usually did, you know, flung up his leg. . . . All at once something went crrr-ack! At first they thought he had torn the cloth of the billiard table, but when they looked, my dear fellow, his United States had split at every seam! He had made such a high kick, the beast, that not a seam was left. . . . Ha-ha-ha, and there were ladies present, too . . . among others the wife of that drivelling Lieutenant Okurin. . . . Okurin was furious. . . . 'How dare the fellow,' said he, 'behave with impropriety in the presence of my wife?' One thing led to another . . . you know our fellows! . . . Okurin sent seconds to Druzhkov, and Druzhkov said 'don't be a fool' . . . ha-ha-ha, 'but tell him he had better send seconds not to me but to the tailor who made me those breeches; it is his fault, you know.' Ha-ha-ha! Ha-ha-ha. . . ."

Lilya and Mila, the colonel's daughters, who were sitting in the window with their round cheeks propped on their fists, flushed crimson and dropped their eyes that looked buried in their plump faces.

"Now you have heard him, haven't you?" Madame Nashatyrin went on, addressing the hotel-keeper. "And that, you consider, of no consequence, I suppose? I am the wife of a colonel, sir! My husband is a commanding officer. I will not permit some cabman to utter such infamies almost in my presence!"

"He is not a cabman, madam, but the staff-captain Kikin. . . . A gentleman born."

"If he has so far forgotten his station as to express himself like a cabman, then he is even more deserving of contempt! In short, don't answer me, but kindly take steps!"

"But what can I do, madam? You are not the only one to complain, everybody's complaining, but what am I to do with him? One goes to his room and begins putting him to shame, saying: 'Hannibal Ivanitch, have some fear of God! It's shameful! and he'll punch you in the face with his fists and say all sorts of things: 'there, put that in your pipe and smoke it,' and such like. It's a disgrace! He wakes up in the morning and sets to walking about the corridor in nothing, saving your presence, but his underclothes. And when he has had a drop he will pick up a revolver and set to putting bullets into the wall. By day he is swilling liquor and at night he plays cards like mad, and after cards it is fighting. . . . I am ashamed for the other lodgers to see it!"

"Why don't you get rid of the scoundrel?"

"Why, there's no getting him out! He owes me for three months, but we don't ask for our money, we simply ask him to get out as a favour . . . . The magistrate has given him an order to clear out of the rooms, but he's taking it from one court to another, and so it drags on. . . . He's a perfect nuisance, that's what he is. And, good Lord, such a man, too! Young, good-looking and intellectual. . . . When he hasn't had a drop you couldn't wish to see a nicer gentleman. The other day he wasn't drunk and he spent the whole day writing letters to his father and mother."

"Poor father and mother!" sighed the colonel's lady.

"They are to be pitied, to be sure! There's no comfort in having such a scamp! He's sworn at and turned out of his lodgings, and not a day passes but he is in trouble over some scandal. It's sad!"

"His poor unhappy wife!" sighed the lady.

"He has no wife, madam. A likely idea! She would have to thank God if her head were not broken. . . ."

The lady walked up and down the room.

"He is not married, you say?"

"Certainly not, madam."

The lady walked up and down the room again and mused a little.

"H'm, not married . . ." she pronounced meditatively. "H'm. Lilya and Mila, don't sit at the window, there's a draught! What a pity! A young man and to let himself sink to this! And all owing to what? The lack of good influence! There is no mother who would. . . . Not married? Well . . . there it is. . . . Please be so good," the lady continued suavely after a moment's thought, "as to go to him and ask him in my name to . . . refrain from using expressions. . . . Tell him that Madame Nashatyrin begs him. . . . Tell him she is staying with her daughters in No. 47 . . . that she has come up from her estate in the country. . . ."

"Certainly."

"Tell him, a colonel's lady and her daughters. He might even come and apologize. . . . We are always at home after dinner. Oh, Mila, shut the window!"

"Why, what do you want with that . . . black sheep, mamma?" drawled Lilya when the hotel-keeper had retired. "A queer person to invite! A drunken, rowdy rascal!"

"Oh, don't say so, ma chere! You always talk like that; and there . . . sit down! Why, whatever he may be, we ought not to despise him. . . . There's something good in everyone. Who knows," sighed the colonel's lady, looking her daughters up and down anxiously, "perhaps your fate is here. Change your dresses anyway. . . ."

IN A STRANGE LAND

SUNDAY, midday. A landowner, called Kamyshev, is sitting in his dining-room, deliberately eating his lunch at a luxuriously furnished table. Monsieur Champoun, a clean, neat, smoothly-shaven, old Frenchman, is sharing the meal with him. This Champoun had once been a tutor in Kamyshev's household, had taught his children good manners, the correct pronunciation of French, and dancing: afterwards when Kamyshev's children had grown up and become lieutenants, Champoun had become something like a *bonne* of the male sex. The duties of the former tutor were not complicated. He had to be properly dressed, to smell of scent, to listen to Kamyshev's idle babble, to eat and drink and sleep - and apparently that was all. For this he received a room, his board, and an indefinite salary.

Kamyshev eats and as usual babbles at random.

"Damnation!" he says, wiping away the tears that have come into his eyes after a mouthful of ham thickly smeared with mustard. "Ough! It has shot into my head and all my joints. Your French mustard would not do that, you know, if you ate the whole potful."

"Some like the French, some prefer the Russian . . ." Champoun assents mildly.

"No one likes French mustard except Frenchmen. And a Frenchman will eat anything, whatever you give him - frogs and rats and black beetles. . . brrr! You don't like that ham, for instance, because it is Russian, but if one were to give you a bit of baked glass and tell you it was French, you would eat it and smack your lips. . . . To your thinking everything Russian is nasty."

"I don't say that."

"Everything Russian is nasty, but if it's French - o say tray zholee! To your thinking there is no country better than France, but to my mind. . . Why, what is France, to tell the truth about it? A little bit of land. Our police captain was sent out there, but in a month he asked to be transferred: there was nowhere to turn round! One can drive round the whole of your France in one day, while here when you drive out of the gate - you can see no end to the land, you can ride on and on. . ."

"Yes, monsieur, Russia is an immense country."

"To be sure it is! To your thinking there are no better people than the French. Well-educated, clever people! Civilization! I agree, the French are all well-educated with elegant manners. . . that is true. . . . A Frenchman never allows himself to be rude: he hands a lady a chair at the right minute, he doesn't eat crayfish with his fork, he doesn't spit on the floor, but . . . there's not the same spirit in him! not the spirit in him! I don't know how to explain it to you but, however one is to express it, there's nothing in a Frenchman of . . . something . . . (the speaker flourishes his fingers) . . . of something . . . fanatical. I remember I have read somewhere that all of you have intelligence acquired from books, while we Russians have innate intelligence. If a Russian studies the sciences properly, none of your French professors is a match for him."

"Perhaps," says Champoun, as it were reluctantly.

"No, not perhaps, but certainly! It's no use your frowning, it's the truth I am speaking. The Russian intelligence is an inventive intelligence. Only of course he is not given a free outlet for it, and he is no hand at boasting. He will invent something - and break it or give it to the children to play with, while your Frenchman will invent some nonsensical thing and make an uproar for all the world to hear it. The other day Iona the coachman carved a little man out of wood, if you pull the little man by a thread he plays unseemly antics. But Iona does not brag of it. . . . I don't like Frenchmen as a rule. I am not referring to you, but speaking generally. . . . They are an immoral people! Outwardly they look like men, but they live like dogs. Take marriage for instance. With us, once you are married, you stick to your wife, and there is no talk about it, but goodness knows how it is with you. The husband is sitting all day long in a cafe, while his wife fills the house with Frenchmen, and sets to dancing the can-can with them."

"That's not true!" Champoun protests, flaring up and unable to restrain himself. "The principle of the family is highly esteemed in France."

"We know all about that principle! You ought to be ashamed to defend it: one ought to be impartial: a pig is always a pig. . . . We must thank the Germans for having beaten them. . . . Yes indeed, God bless them for it."

"In that case, monsieur, I don't understand. . ." says the Frenchman leaping up with flashing eyes, "if you hate the French why do you keep me?"

"What am I to do with you?"

"Let me go, and I will go back to France."

"Wha-at? But do you suppose they would let you into France now? Why, you are a traitor to your country! At one time Napoleon's your great man, at another Gambetta. . . . Who the devil can make you out?"

"Monsieur," says Champoun in French, spluttering and crushing up his table napkin in his hands, "my worst enemy could not have thought of a greater insult than the outrage you have just done to my feelings! All is over!"

And with a tragic wave of his arm the Frenchman flings his dinner napkin on the table majestically, and walks out of the room with dignity.

Three hours later the table is laid again, and the servants bring in the dinner. Kamyshev sits alone at the table. After the preliminary glass he feels a craving to babble. He wants to chatter, but he has no listener.

"What is Alphonse Ludovikovitch doing?" he asks the footman.

"He is packing his trunk, sir."

"What a noodle! Lord forgive us!" says Kamyshev, and goes in to the Frenchman.

Champoun is sitting on the floor in his room, and with trembling hands is packing in his trunk his linen, scent bottles, prayer-books, braces, ties. . . . All his correct figure, his trunk, his bedstead and the table - all have an air of elegance and effeminacy. Great tears are dropping from his big blue eyes into the trunk.

"Where are you off to?" asks Kamyshev, after standing still for a little.

The Frenchman says nothing.

"Do you want to go away?" Kamyshev goes on. "Well, you know, but . . . I won't venture to detain you. But what is queer is, how are you going to travel without a passport? I wonder! You know I have lost your passport. I thrust it in somewhere between some papers, and it is lost. . . . And they are strict about passports among us. Before you have gone three or four miles they pounce upon you."

Champoun raises his head and looks mistrustfully at Kamyshev.

"Yes. . . . You will see! They will see from your face you haven't a passport, and ask at once: Who is that? Alphonse Champoun. We know that Alphonse Champoun. Wouldn't you like to go under police escort somewhere nearer home!"

"Are you joking?"

"What motive have I for joking? Why should I? Only mind now; it's a compact, don't you begin whining then and writing letters. I won't stir a finger when they lead

Anton Chekhov

you by in fetters!"

Champoun jumps up and, pale and wide-eyed, begins pacing up and down the room.

"What are you doing to me?" he says in despair, clutching at his head. "My God! accursed be that hour when the fatal thought of leaving my country entered my head! . . ."

"Come, come, come . . . I was joking!" says Kamyshev in a lower tone. "Queer fish he is; he doesn't understand a joke. One can't say a word!"

"My dear friend!" shrieks Champoun, reassured by Kamyshev's tone. "I swear I am devoted to Russia, to you and your children. . . . To leave you is as bitter to me as death itself! But every word you utter stabs me to the heart!"

"Ah, you queer fish! If I do abuse the French, what reason have you to take offence? You are a queer fish really! You should follow the example of Lazar Isaakitch, my tenant. I call him one thing and another, a Jew, and a scurvy rascal, and I make a pig's ear out of my coat tail, and catch him by his Jewish curls. He doesn't take offence."

"But he is a slave! For a kopeck he is ready to put up with any insult!"

"Come, come, come . . . that's enough! Peace and concord!"

Champoun powders his tear-stained face and goes with Kamyshev to the dining-room. The first course is eaten in silence, after the second the same performance begins over again, and so Champoun's sufferings have no end.

Anton Chekhov

Choose from Thousands of 1stWorldLibrary Classics By

A. M. Barnard
Ada Leverson
Adolphus William Ward
Aesop
Agatha Christie
Alexander Aaronsohn
Alexander Kielland
Alexandre Dumas
Alfred Gatty
Alfred Ollivant
Alice Duer Miller
Alice Turner Curtis
Alice Dunbar
Ambrose Bierce
Amelia E. Barr
Amory H. Bradford
Andrew Lang
Andrew McFarland Davis
Andy Adams
Anna Sewell
Annie Besant
Annie Hamilton Donnell
Annie Payson Call
Annonaymous
Anton Chekhov
Arnold Bennett
Arthur Conan Doyle
Arthur M. Winfield
Arthur Ransome
Atticus
B.H. Baden-Powell
B. M. Bower
Baroness Emmuska Orczy
Baroness Orczy
Basil King
Bayard Taylor
Ben Macomber
Bertha Muzzy Bower
Bjornstjerne Bjornson
Booth Tarkington
Boyd Cable
Bram Stoker
C. Collodi
C. E. Orr
C. M. Ingleby
Carolyn Wells
Catherine Parr Traill
Charles A. Eastman
Charles Dickens

Charles Dudley Warner
Charles Farrar Browne
Charles Ives
Charles Kingsley
Charles Klein
Charles Amory Beach
Charles Hanson Towne
Charles Lathrop Pack
Charles Whibley
Charles Willing Beale
Charlotte M. Braeme
Charlotte M. Yonge
Charlotte Perkins Stetson
Clair W. Hayes
Clarence Day Jr.
Clarence E. Mulford
Clemence Housman
Confucius
Cornelis DeWitt Wilcox
Cyril Burleigh
D. H. Lawrence
Daniel Defoe
David Garnett
Dinah Craik
Don Carlos Janes
Donald Keyhoe
Dorothy Kilner
Dougan Clark
Douglas Fairbanks
E. Nesbit
E.P.Roe
E. Phillips Oppenheim
Earl Barnes
Edgar Rice Burroughs
Edith Van Dyne
Edith Wharton
Edward J. O'Biren
Edward S. Ellis
Edwin L. Arnold
Eleanor Atkins
Eliot Gregory
Elizabeth Gaskell
Elizabeth McCracken
Elizabeth Von Arnim
Ellem Key
Emerson Hough
Emilie F. Carlen
Emily Dickinson
Enid Bagnold

Enilor Macartney Lane
Erasmus W. Jones
Ernie Howard Pie
Ethel Turner
Ethel Watts Mumford
Eugenie Foa
Eugene Wood
Eustace Hale Ball
Evelyn Everett-green
Everard Cotes
F. H. Cheley
F. J. Cross
Federick Austin Ogg
Ferdinand Ossendowski
Francis Bacon
Francis Darwin
Frances Hodgson Burnett
Frances Parkinson Keyes
Frank Gee Patchin
Frank Harris
Frank Jewett Mather
Frank L. Packard
Frank V. Webster
Frederic Stewart Isham
Frederick Trevor Hill
Frederick Winslow Taylor
Friedrich Kerst
Friedrich Nietzsche
Fyodor Dostoyevsky
G.A. Henty
G.K. Chesterton
Gabrielle E. Jackson
Garrett P. Serviss
Gaston Leroux
George A. Warren
George Ade
Geroge Bernard Shaw
George Durston
George Ebers
George Eliot
George Gissing
George MacDonald
George Meredith
George Orwell
George Sylvester Viereck
George Tucker
George W. Cable
George Wharton James
Gertrude Atherton

Grace E. King	J. Henri Fabre	Katherine Stokes
Grace Gallatin	J. M. Barrie	L. A. Abbot
Grant Allen	J. Macdonald Oxley	L. T. Meade
Guillermo A. Sherwell	J. S. Fletcher	L. Frank Baum
Gulielma Zollinger	J. S. Knowles	Latta Griswold
Gustav Flaubert	J. Storer Clouston	Laura Lee Hope
H. A. Cody	Jack London	Laurence Housman
H. B. Irving	Jacob Abbott	Lawrence Beasley
H.C. Bailey	James Allen	Leo Tolstoy
H. G. Wells	James Andrews	Leonid Andreyev
H. H. Munro	James Baldwin	Lewis Carroll
H. Irving Hancock	James DeMille	Lewis Sperry Chafer
H. Rider Haggard	James Joyce	Lilian Bell
H. W. C. Davis	James Lane Allen	Lloyd Osbourne
Hamilton Wright Mabie	James Lane Allen	Louis Hughes
Hans Christian Andersen	James Oliver Curwood	Louis Tracy
Harold Avery	James Oppenheim	Louisa May Alcott
Harold McGrath	James Otis	Lucy Fitch Perkins
Harriet Beecher Stowe	James R. Driscoll	Lucy Maud Montgomery
Harry Houidini	Jane Austen	Lydia Miller Middleton
Helent Hunt Jackson	Janet Aldridge	Lyndon Orr
Helen Nicolay	Jens Peter Jacobsen	M. Corvus
Hendrik Conscience	Jerome K. Jerome	M. H. Adams
Hendy David Thoreau	John Burroughs	Margaret E. Sangster
Henri Barbusse	John Cournos	Margaret Vandercook
Henrik Ibsen	John F. Kennedy	Margret Penrose
Henry Adams	John Gay	Maria Edgeworth
Henry Ford	John Glasworthy	Maria Thompson Daviess
Henry Frost	John Habberton	Mariano Azuela
Henry James	John Joy Bell	Marion Polk Angellotti
Henry Jones Ford	John Kendrick Bangs	Mark Overton
Henry Seton Merriman	John Milton	Mark Twain
Henry W Longfellow	John Philip Sousa	Mary Austin
Herbert A. Giles	Jonas Lauritz Idemil Lie	Mary Catherine Crowley
Herbert N. Casson	Jonathan Swift	Mary Cole
Herman Hesse	Joseph A. Altsheler	Mary Hastings Bradley
Homer	Joseph Carey	Mary Roberts Rinehart
Honore De Balzac	Joseph Conrad	Mary Rowlandson
Horace Walpole	Joseph E. Badger Jr	M. Wollstonecraft Shelley
Horatio Alger Jr.	Joseph Hergesheimer	Maud Lindsay
Howard Pyle	Joseph Jacobs	Max Beerbohm
Howard R. Garis	Jules Vernes	Myra Kelly
Hugh Lofting	Julian Hawthrone	Nathaniel Hawthrone
Hugh Walpole	Julie A Lippmann	Nicolo Machiavelli
Humphry Ward	Justin Huntly McCarthy	O. F. Walton
Ian Maclaren	Kakuzo Okakura	Oscar Wilde
Inez Haynes Gillmore	Kenneth Grahame	Owen Johnson
Irving Bacheller	Kenneth McGaffey	P.G. Wodehouse
Israel Abrahams	Kate Langley Bosher	Paul and Mabel Thorne
Ivan Turgenev	Kate Langley Bosher	Paul G. Tomlinson
J.G.Austin	Katherine Cecil Thurston	Paul Severing

Percy Brebner
Peter B. Kyne
Plato
R. Derby Holmes
R. L. Stevenson
R. S. Ball
Rabindranath Tagore
Rahul Alvares
Ralph Bonehill
Ralph Henry Barbour
Ralph Victor
Ralph Waldo Emmerson
Rene Descartes
Rex Beach
Rex E. Beach
Richard Harding Davis
Richard Jefferies
Richard Le Gallienne
Robert Barr
Robert Frost
Robert Gordon Anderson
Robert L. Drake
Robert Lansing
Robert Lynd
Robert Michael Ballantyne
Robert W. Chambers
Rosa Nouchette Carey
Rudyard Kipling
Samuel B. Allison
Samuel Hopkins Adams
Sarah Bernhardt
Sarah C. Hallowell
Selma Lagerlof
Sherwood Anderson
Sigmund Freud
Standish O'Grady
Stanley Weyman
Stella Benson
Stephen Crane
Stewart Edward White
Stijn Streuvels
Swami Abhedananda
Swami Parmananda
T. S. Ackland
T. S. Arthur
The Princess Der Ling
Thomas A. Janvier
Thomas A Kempis
Thomas Anderton
Thomas Bailey Aldrich
Thomas Bulfinch

Thomas De Quincey
Thomas H. Huxley
Thomas Hardy
Thomas More
Thornton W. Burgess
U. S. Grant
Valentine Williams
Various Authors
Vaughan Kester
Victor Appleton
Virginia Woolf
Walter Camp
Walter Scott
Washington Irving
Wilbur Lawton
Wilkie Collins
Willa Cather
Willard F. Baker
William Dean Howells
William le Queux
W. Makepeace Thackeray
William W. Walter
Winston Churchill
Yei Theodora Ozaki
Yogi Ramacharaka
Young E. Allison
Zane Grey